T0209083

BENEATH THE CRESCENT MOON

LOUIS J. CUCCIA

iUniverse®

BENEATH THE CRESCENT MOON

This is a work of fiction. All the characters, names, incidents, organizations, and dialogue in this novel are either the products of the author's imagination or are used fictitiously.

Cover illustration and Two-Faced Wolf credited to: Abby Rose McCormack
Bible Verses credited to New American Bible, New York, New York, 1970

iUniverse books may be ordered through booksellers or by contacting:

iUniverse
1663 Liberty Drive
Bloomington, IN 47403
www.iuniverse.com
844-349-9409

ISBN: 978-1-6632-1165-1 (sc)
ISBN: 978-1-6632-1268-9 (hc)
ISBN: 978-1-6632-1386-0 (e)

Library of Congress Control Number: 2020923371

Print information available on the last page.

iUniverse rev. date: 12/04/2020

BENEATH THE CRESCENT MOON
LIES THE GARDEN OF STONE

Amid the garden lie only the memories of the gardeners. Time has stopped. Only beginnings and endings remain—dates etched in marble and stone. What of the time between? Is there nothing left behind in this emptiness of time? Some dates span a generation and others only one day. But each stone flower has its place in the garden, carefully grouped by the gardeners. Time starts again, leaving behind the gardeners to weep of the vacancy in time.

> But the souls of the just are in the hand of God,
> and no torment shall touch them.
> They seemed, in the view of the foolish, to be dead;
> and their passing away was thought an affliction
> and their going from us, utter destruction;
> But they are in peace.
> For if before men, indeed, they be punished,
> yet in their hope full of immortality;
> Chastised a little, they shall be greatly blessed,
> because God tried them and found them worthy of himself.
> As gold in the furnace, he proved them,
> and as a sacrificial offering he took them to himself.
> —Wisdom 3:1–6

PREFACE

In 1718, there was need for a trade town that could be reached from both Lake Pontchartrain and the Mississippi River, and a spot was chosen. The town became known as La Nouvelle-Orléans.

In 1762, France passed ownership of the Louisiana Territory to Spain in the Treaty of Fontainebleau. Then, in 1800, the territory was given back to Napoleon of France in the secret Treaty of San Ildefonso. It wasn't until 1803 that the land would belong to America with the Louisiana Purchase under the leadership of President Thomas Jefferson. The land deal of $15 million comprised some six hundred million acres and stretched from the Mississippi River to the Pacific Ocean.

Today La Nouvelle-Orléans, the crescent-shaped city built at a sharp bend in the Mississippi River, is known as New Orleans.

When I think of New Orleans, I think of jazz and Cajun music, including Louis Armstrong, Louis Prima, and Kate Smith; Mardi Gras; Bourbon Street and the French Quarter; and New Orleans food favorites, such as red beans and rice, beignets, chicory-laced coffee, backyard crawfish boils, jambalaya, king cake, and Italian pastries from Brocato's Bakery, all of which are entangled among the historic sights of wrought iron balconies, the St. Louis Cathedral, Jackson Square, shotgun houses, and Café Du Monde. This is New Orleans.

Many of these images of New Orleans—the beautiful cathedrals, churches, gardens, courtyards, cemeteries, and stonework—are from the 1700s. They were adopted when the French colonists first lay claim to the swampy lands, and they still adorn the majestic city. Venturing out along the concrete walk by the Mississippi River gives me a feeling of belonging to a historic area populated with immigrants. In this melting pot of the South, one can enjoy the conversation and culture of the French, Cajun, Italian, African, German, American Indian, Irish, Polish, Arcadian, and Spanish.

The true beauty of this city derives not from its architecture or history but from the blending of the cultures of its people. This multicultural group has stood against hurricanes, flooding, epidemics, and fire and fought control by Britain in the Battle of New Orleans in 1814.

As with most large cities, New Orleans has its dark side. The crime rate is one of the highest in the United States. Political corruption, mishandling of government funds, and favoritism have plagued the city since the days of Huey Long. Even today, the practice of voodoo, superstition, and ghost stories persist throughout the city. From the famous queen of voodoo, Marie Laveau, to the haunted houses, mansions, and cemeteries, New Orleans is called the most haunted city in America.

With all its darkness, the richness of this city can still be found today at every local merchant, church, coffeehouse, backyard cookout, music bar, bakery, and restaurant. This is my New Orleans, a city of mystery and enchantment, beauty and hope.

New Orleans Police Department
News Release

Homicide in Metairie

February 2, 2018, 11:55 a.m.

18-76159

On Thursday, February 1, 2018, at approximately 6:45 a.m., the New Orleans Police Department responded to the call of a deceased subject found in a car at the Grand Mart Motel, 8006 W. Metairie Drive, in Metairie. Upon arrival, officers found a deceased female. New Orleans Police Department officers and investigators conducted interviews and collected evidence at the scene.

On Friday, February 2, 2018, additional interviews were conducted at the New Orleans Police Department Investigations Division. The interviews resulted in the recovery of additional information and evidence. There has been no arrest currently.

The identity of the deceased is being withheld until next of kin has been notified.

If you have any information regarding this crime, please contact Detective Dominic DeAngelis at the New Orleans Investigations Division: 504-335-7888, extension 442.

CHAPTER 1

A Louisiana deputy stands by the black metal door that allows prisoners in and out of the gray cinder block room at the New Orleans Parish Prison. I sit and watch from outside the glass enclosure as a prisoner shuffles into the room. His ankle fetters make an eerie scraping noise as they slide across the dusty concrete floor. The sound makes my skin crawl, like someone dragging his fingernails down a chalkboard. My muscles quiver uncontrollably for a microsecond, and I feel prickly bumps flush on my arms. A dwarflike shadow, distorted by the overhead light, slowly moves across the block wall. As the silhouette falls off the wall onto the floor, Raymond Lester Morone takes a seat behind enclosure number three. His lifeless face droops in silence.

Picking up my paired phone, I wait for a connection on the other side. Raymond's head slowly rises until our eyes meet. Sunken cheeks and protruding face bones declare major weight loss. Stringy dark hair drapes over his ears and shines as if smeared with baby oil. His unshaven face and bloodshot eyes reflect a tale of sleep deprivation. His orange jumpsuit contrasts his ivory skin. A large bruise with yellow edges accents the back of his right forearm. Another one covers the back of his left hand. I judge Raymond to be around my height—a little less than six feet tall—and maybe 140 pounds. It's hard to tell with his oversize clothing and slumped position. Trembling cuffed hands pick up the phone. Spindly fingers tipped with blackened nails place it to his ear.

"Mr. Morone, my name is Justin Lancer. I'm an investigative reporter for the *New Orleans Chronicle*. I have read the recent articles in the *Daily News Journal* and wanted to follow up on the information that was presented. Will you talk to me about what happened?"

Raymond looks up at me. His mouth quivers as if he's trying to speak, and he drops his eyes. He repositions himself in the plastic chair. He glances back at the guard and, after a minute, returns to reality. "Can you help me?"

The news article runs through my mind. Raymond Lester Morone, age thirty-seven, was arrested for suspicion of several murders in the New Orleans area. All were young women in their thirties. All were found in their cars after working late, and all died of strangulation. The first victim was a late-night motel clerk in Metairie. One was a nurse at Picayune General Hospital. Another worked at a twenty-four-hour market in Kenner, near Louis Armstrong Airport.

The article stated that Raymond was arrested at two o'clock in the morning on April 21, 2018. Until the day he was arrested, Raymond seemingly led a normal life. His arrest has revealed more questions than answers. No records can be found. According to the police, Raymond doesn't exist. At the time of his arrest, he had a fake ID and a copy of an Alabama vehicle registration, also fake. He claims he graduated from Delgado Community College, Slidell Campus, in St. Tammany Parish, and received his Bachelor of Arts in 2005, at the age of twenty-two. Delgado has no record of Raymond Lester Morone. He never married and, for the last three years, has worked as a handyman. His last known address is an apartment on Esplanade.

Raymond turns to stare at the blank gray cinder wall, as if frozen in time.

"Raymond? Raymond, talk to me. I will do all I can to help, but you have to talk to me."

Raymond slowly turns his head back toward me and makes eye contact. "They say they're going to send me to the Farm and fry me."

"Who, Raymond? Who said that?"

"One of them," he says, motioning toward the jailer. "They say my brain will cook."

I visited the Louisiana State Penitentiary, known as Angola, back in 2006. That was the year I received my BS in criminal justice from LSU at the age of twenty-four. The penitentiary is often referred to as the Alcatraz of the South or the Farm. Angola is the largest maximum-security prison in the United States. It houses more than 6,300 prisoners and 1,800 staff. It is located in West Feliciana Parish and is surrounded on three sides by water. The eighteen-thousand-acre piece of land the prison sits on was known before the American Civil War as the Angola Plantations and was owned by Isaac Franklin. The prison is located at the end of Louisiana Highway 66, around twenty-two miles northwest of St. Francisville. It's about an hour's drive from Baton Rouge and two hours from New Orleans. Death row for men and the state execution chamber for both sexes are located at the Angola facility.

"Raymond, listen to me. I can't promise anything, but if you will talk to me, I'll do all I can to help you. Will you do that?"

Raymond stares down at the floor, and I can hear the fetters around his ankles drag on the concrete. "They tell me I will get a public defender in court. Is that true?"

"That's true. But don't you have some family who can hire an attorney for you? You need more help than just an appointed defender."

"No. Nobody. No family anymore." Raymond stares off into space and remains silent, as if trying to evaluate his position.

"Raymond, you need someone to help investigate your case. A public defender won't spend the time investigating like I will. He's tied up with dozens of cases. If you will give me your side of the story, I'll trace back each incident. You need some outside help. And if you'll sign over the rights to your story, my service will cost you nothing. Will you do that?"

Raymond looks down as if inspecting the bruise on his right

forearm. Seconds tick by in silence. "Do you think I killed those women?"

"Did you?"

Raymond leans forward and moves closer to the glass partition. His bloodshot eyes contact mine. "I did not."

His stare never changes. No blink and no nerve movement in the eyebrows. The stare is so strong that I feel an uneasiness in my stomach. I've interviewed a lot of people over the years, and I consider myself good at reading faces. This man either is telling me the truth or is the best damn liar I've ever met.

I force a smile to break the tension. "Then you need my help. Think it over. I'm offering you a chance for free help. I'm only allowed to visit once per week. You must let me know something if you want my help, so I can get started. Can I call on you next week? You okay with that?"

Without answering, Raymond places the receiver back in its cradle. He stands up and motions to the deputy that he's through. Starting to leave the enclosure, Raymond turns back toward me and mumbles, "Next week."

On the way back from the prison, I get a call from Cindy, the *New Orleans Chronicle's* secretary, informing me that Rocco wants me back at the paper ASAP. Rocco Donalli has been running the *New Orleans Chronicle* since 2006. Somewhere along the way, the original owners got into a large lawsuit over some political information that was released to the public concerning city officials. Some were accused of mishandling funds earmarked for Hurricane Katrina victims. Shortly before the court date, there was a settlement. The suit was dropped, the original owners ended up with an estate in northern Italy, and Rocco suddenly appeared from nowhere as the new owner.

Rocco appears to be in his late fifties, never has married, and has a demanding personality. Maybe he's a little more than demanding. Maybe *hard ass* is a better description. To me, Rocco looks like a taller

Danny DeVito, with the same balding, wild black hair attached to an oversize head and a squatty five-and-a-half-foot body. His hairy Popeye forearms stick out of an always-too-small shirt whose buttons seem to scream in pain as they stretch over his watermelon-sized belly. His dark black mustache hangs over his upper lip, and he is never without a Parodi cigarillo, a black cigarillo made in the USA from the dark-fired tobaccos of Kentucky and Tennessee. The cigarillos' strong horse-dung aroma saturates his office and clothes.

After my graduation from LSU, I joined the Army and entered Officer Candidate School and later 95 Bravo, the MOS designation for the military police. Once I was discharged from the army, I took a couple of have-to-eat jobs before ending up at the *Chronicle* in 2011. The *NOLA Chronicle*, as it is often called, is like most tabloids found at grocery store checkout lines.

Tom and Candy Kuyendall, the original owners, started the business in 1959 and ran it until selling out to Rocco Donalli in 2006. Rocco's challenge was to rebuild the failing post-Katrina *Chronicle* and put it back in the black. He did just that. Rocco has a knack for emphasis on local politics and crime. In just five years, he brought the paper's circulation to around ten thousand copies a week, and it is now the largest tabloid in the state of Louisiana.

My job is to turn in my investigative reports directly to Rocco. He then takes a little liberty—sometimes more than a little—and puts the final spin on the story before it goes to print. It bothers me when the stories change to meet the demand of the readers, but the work is steady, it pays well, and NOLA is never lacking in stories about crime and politics.

Following Tulane east, I work my way to South Carrollton Avenue and head north toward City Park. After turning left onto Dumaine Street, I turn into the *Chronicle*'s parking lot. As I enter the front door, Cindy motions for me to go straight into Rocco's office.

As I walk into his office, Rocco is leaning back in his chair with a phone to his ear and an unlit Parodi hanging off his lower lip. His ashtray has several butts in it, surrounded by three cups of coffee and a can of Mountain Dew. He points at the chair in front of his desk and continues to talk.

"I'm sending Justin Lancer by to talk to you about the Morone case." After a short pause, he continues. "Yeah, yeah, I get it, but you owe me big-time, and I'm calling in my debt." There's another pause. "Listen to me, Dominic. I can assure you that your name will never be mentioned, and whatever information you can give us will be greatly appreciated. And I mean greatly. Capisce?" Rocco's smile expands as he listens to the reply. "Where and when?" He picks up one of the many pens spread over his desk and makes a note. "Grazie, amico mio. Dopo."

Hanging up the phone, he turns his attention toward me. "You'd better have some good news for me, kid, as I just got you an interview with one of the detectives who was involved in the Morone case. Don't make me look stupid. Did you get the interview with Morone?"

"I did. He agreed to talk to me next week." I look at the man across the desk. His shirt looks as if he's worn it for more than a week. I've always been amazed by how many people Rocco knows and how he gets his hooks into them.

He tears off the sticky note from the pad and hands me the information. "You can meet Dominic DeAngelis at two o'clock at the Acme Oyster House in Covington. You know the place?"

"Yes, been there many times. Great place to wind down."

"Well, get your butt over there. Dominic is off today and is looking for some beer and oysters."

"How will I know him?"

Rocco looks over the top of his black-rimmed glasses. "If you can't find an Italian cop by the name of Dominic DeAngelis at two o'clock in the afternoon in an oyster bar, you're fired. Now, get the hell out of my office."

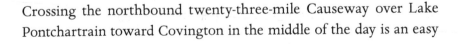

Crossing the northbound twenty-three-mile Causeway over Lake Pontchartrain toward Covington in the middle of the day is an easy ride. The two parallel concrete structures were constructed in the 1950s and '60s. The Causeway connects New Orleans, by way of Metairie with Mandeville, and bisects the lake in a northeast line. Lake Pontchartrain is a brackish estuary connected to the Gulf of Mexico. North of the lake are the Northshore and St. Tammany Parish. Covington is the parish seat.

Peering over the side of the bridge, I can see several small fishing boats struggling to maintain position as small whitecaps roll on the dark water. The wind is a huge factor as it blows unobstructed across the bridge and lake. On windy days, traffic alerts are plastered on the steel overhead poles of the bridge. In high-wind situations, the bridge is closed to traffic.

Over the choppy waters, flocks of birds circle, searching for bait fish. A light brown pelican glides alongside the bridge, looking for a resting spot in the afternoon sun. Traffic slows as the Northshore draws near, and I approach the exit ramp in Mandeville. Continuing north on Highway 190, I pass under Interstate 12 into Covington.

A quick glance around the Acme Oyster House parking lot reveals ten cars and a couple of motorcycles. Monday afternoon is not a busy time of day for the oyster bar. Upon entering the bar, I'm immediately struck by the smell of seafood and the sound of Cajun music. Off to the left of the bar is a table occupied by four men. Empty beer bottles and plates of oyster shells fill the tabletop. Tattooed arms suspended in the air slap high-five as the men's laughter exceeds the music. Several couples sit along the bar, in modest chatter. To the right, two guys with do-rags and Duck Commander–style beards clink their beer bottles before sucking them dry.

In the far corner sits Dominic. There's no question. A huge man with dark skin raises his beer to get my attention. Dwarfing the table, Dominic looks to be every inch of six foot seven and 250 pounds. His graying black hair and sun-beaten skin give him the appearance of being in his midfifties. His blue-and-red Hawaiian shirt is unbuttoned halfway down his chest, exposing an unruly mass of hair. As I approach his table, I can see a faded Marine tattoo on his left forearm. The man's whole demeanor says, "Don't mess with me."

I sit down and look at an empty Abita Turbodog beer bottle in the middle of the table and a full one in front of me.

"I started you a tab. Barbecued shrimp and a dozen oysters on the way." Dominic smiles and takes a swig of beer. "Rocco says you're a pretty good investigator. You look to be midthirties. Six feet tall. Hundred sixty pounds. College boy. Maybe top of your class. Above-average build, so I figure you work out during the week. No tats but a military cut. Well groomed, pressed clothes, and straight teeth. Means you came from a middle- or upper-class family. Probably grew up in the Big Easy."

The Big Easy is one of the many nicknames given to NOLA. If I recall my NOLA history correctly, there was a dance hall in New Orleans called the Big Easy back in the 1900s. In the 1970s, a newspaper reporter started calling New Orleans by this name. She compared the easy-going way of life here to the hurried pace of life in New York City.

Nicknames help establish the identity of a city. They can also spread pride among its citizens. New Orleans probably has more nicknames than any other American city. In 1970, James Conaway wrote a crime novel called *The Big Easy*.

A waiter interrupts Dominic and sets down two trays. "Anything else?"

"Yeah, mix me a little bowl of hot sauce and horseradish, half and half. Bring a spoon along with it," replies Dominic as he motions with his beer for a refill.

The waiter picks up the empty beer bottle and looks over at me. I shake my head in reply.

Dominic waits for the waiter to leave and then continues. "Don't really like giving a noose to somebody I don't know, so let's me and you play a little game. Tell me about the two guys at the table with the beards. What did you notice when you walked in?"

His voice has a low, gravelly tone. His accent sounds more Cajun than Italian. He leans back in his chair and waits for my answer. He knows how to play cop. Once you ask a question, you remain silent. If you speak before you get an answer, you lose. I must admit Dominic is about to piss me off. He's playing games with the wrong guy. I want to give him my name, rank, and serial number and walk out, but I need to find out what he knows. My other option is to turn the tables.

"The first thing I noticed in the parking lot was a dark blue Taurus parked on the side all by itself. I thought to myself, *The owner of that car must be a loner.* It looks in fairly good shape, so it might be owned by someone who was in the service. As a matter of fact, there's a Marine sticker on the back windshield and a vertical dent on the back bumper. Maybe it's owned by someone who drank too much one night and backed into a pole. The one thing I can't figure out is where its hubcaps are. I don't know if somebody stole them or the owner lost them somewhere."

Dominic quickly turns his body around to look at his car through the window. As soon as he sees his hubcaps, he knows he's been had. He sheepishly turns back to face me and smiles. I raise my beer as a cheer and take a swig.

"I like you, kid. You've got guts."

"The name is Justin. If you want my résumé, you're out of luck, and I'll tell Rocco you changed your mind."

The waiter interrupts again and drops off the bowl of sauce and another beer.

"No, no, we're good. Sometimes I forget I'm off duty." Dominic leans in and pushes the oyster tray toward me, offering a token of peace. "Best oysters in NOLA area. Get you some." The table with the two bearded men gets loud, and I hear glass break and laughter behind my back. Dominic looks over but doesn't seem alarmed.

"You got my back?" I ask, picking up an oyster shell and smiling at Dominic.

"No problem," Dominic replies. "You packing?"

"Kel-Tec .380. Never leave home without it. By the way, the one on the right has a blue do-rag with the name Dog on it. He is wearing a gold chain around his neck and has a skull ring on his left hand. White T-shirt, open black vest, blue jeans, and black boots with a chrome strip on the toe. The one on the left has a red do-rag with white crossbones. He has a leather clip in his beard, black T-shirt, no vest, and blue jeans with a tear on the right knee. Gold ring on his left pinkie finger.

Black boots with the leather worn off the toes. Bikes out front have Mississippi tags. Both Harleys, one red and one blue." I suck an oyster down and take another swig of beer.

Dominic breaks into a grin from ear to ear. "I knew I liked you."

The waiter throws a towel at the bikers. "Clean it up, Dog. This is the last time I'm telling you: no stacking beer bottles or glasses."

Dog lets out a roar of laughter as he looks at the towel on the floor. "Take it easy, man. We were just leaving. Drop me a tab."

The waiter brings a bill and waits.

"What's the matter, Slim? You having a bad hair day?" Dog pulls out some cash and throws it onto the table. "Keep the change." The two bikers get up, laughing, and exit the front door. I can hear the Harleys as they start up and drive off from the parking lot.

Dominic and I talk for another thirty minutes. He mostly makes small talk about NOLA and the police force. His conversation stays away from discussing the Morone case. The waiter drops by again, and Dominic asks for the bill—or, should I say, my bill. Once the bill is dropped off, Dominic leans forward and lowers his voice. "Just how much do you know about the case?"

"Just what I've read in the papers. I contacted Morone, and he agreed to talk with me next week. I'm trying to gather all the background information I can to determine if what he tells me is true and how good his memory is."

"Well, I'll tell you what I know. If you find that he's open with you, we can meet again. If he's feeding you a bunch of crap, case closed."

"I'm good with that. Is there anything you can tell me that's not included in the reports? Names, places, or dates you're aware of that didn't make it to the department?"

"First victim's name is Elizabeth Mary DeBoy. White female. Age thirty-nine. She had worked at the motel for about four months. Lived by herself in an apartment on Bayou Lane in Slidell, near Olde Town Center. No boyfriend, both parents died in 2002, and no prior records. Seems to have lived a normal life. Kept to herself. Didn't share much with her coworkers at the motel."

"Anybody see or hear anything the night of the murder?" I ask.

"I'd check on a guy named William Sutton. Goes by Viper. He's one of those goth-dressing millennials. Long black coat; black painted fingernails and lips; long, greasy hair—you know the type. Has tats on most of his body, including a snake with two heads on his neck. He claims to have seen Morone at the motel the night of the first murder. Hangs out at the Cave on Northshore. Usually there most nights. Smokes a little grass but no hard stuff. Says he was meeting someone at the motel, when he saw Morone. He gave me some good info, so I let him slide. He's worth more to me on the outside than the inside. Tell him Dominic sent you. He should be open to talking with you."

"What about video surveillance?"

"Nothing. Cameras are just there for looks."

After paying the bill, I bid Dominic goodbye. Feeling a little light-headed from the Turbodog, I decide to go home and get some coffee.

Heading south on Highway 190, I pick up Interstate 12, heading east toward Slidell. Southeast of Slidell, on the east side of Lake Pontchartrain and Highway 90, is Lake Catherine. I often remember the day my parents and I evacuated NOLA and headed north on I-59 to stay with friends in Hattiesburg, Mississippi. My parents lived on Lake Catherine, in a cabin just off Bay Jaune, until 2005. That was the year Hurricane Katrina devastated New Orleans and washed away their property.

The storm hit New Orleans as a category-five hurricane and led to fifty-three levee breaches. Flooding was estimated to have affected as much as 80 percent of the city, and the estimated death count ranged from 1,000 to 1,500. Most of the major roads were damaged, and a large portion of the I-10 Twin Span Bridge traveling toward Slidell collapsed. It was estimated that a little more than one million of the 1.3 million residents evacuated. Two sections of the waterproof-membrane roof of the Superdome, which was sheltering approximately twenty-six thousand people who had not evacuated, were peeled off.

It was a month before we could get back. The house's support poles were the only thing standing. Nothing else remained. Dad and I had worked hard on the property for many years before Katrina. We had extended the pier and added lights for night fishing, hoping to bring in enough speckled trout for a late-night supper. We had worked together several weekends to screen in the back porch, pour a concrete pad, and build a wood deck. The last year before Katrina, we'd added a fire pit and picnic tables for our crawfish boils. On the day we were able to return, the whole site was gone. We were crushed. Tired of the broken promises and political corruption of some city officials, Dad sold the land and found a nice place in Baton Rouge.

After arriving home, I make a pot of coffee and step outside into the backyard. I sit at a wood picnic table under a covered deck as the afternoon sun throws shadows across the grass. Late-April temperatures in NOLA usually range in the eighties, with 80 percent humidity. This day is no different. Enjoying the afternoon heat, a gecko sits on the wood fence that surrounds my property. He tilts his head back and forth, assessing the area for predators and food. Bees hover over the wildflowers that seem to take over the side landscaping every summer. The smell of honeysuckle permeates the sticky air.

I recall the evenings when Kate and I would sit here for hours, just talking about whatever came to mind. I met Kate Ehlers while attending LSU. After graduation, we kept in touch when I left for the army, and she entered the School of the Art Institute of Chicago and received her master of fine arts degree. When I returned, we picked up where we had left off. By then, Kate had started her own media company specializing in magazine photography. She now travels all over the world, taking photos in Africa, France, New Zealand, and Russia. At one time, we talked about marriage, but with her schedule, the time didn't seem right for us.

My cell phone rings, and I look at Kate's name on the caller ID and wonder if my thoughts transmitted her response.

"Hey, babe, how are things in NOLA?" asks Kate.

"Good here. Hot and humid. How is Hawaii?" I ask. Kate is on another trip for *National Geographic*, shooting photos of Kilauea, the volcano located along the southern shore of the Big Island.

"It's beautiful here, and Kilauea is awesome. I'm able to be flown over for my photos in a helicopter. You can feel the heat as you get closer to the smoke column. I'll probably be here another couple of weeks. Wish you could be here to share the sunsets on the ocean. It's so peaceful. Maybe we can take some time off this winter. I'd love to spend some free time here."

"You know, I'd love that too. Let's plan on it."

"I'll check my schedule when I get home, and we'll set a date."

There is that word again: schedule. *All I can do is hope.* "Sounds good, Kate. I'm all in."

"Got to run. Love you, babe, and call you later."

"Love you too. Be careful, and get some good pics." The phone goes dead in my hands. Maybe one day, when the stars align, we'll find each other again. But right now, I must get ready for a late-night trip to the Cave to see if I can locate Viper.

CHAPTER 2

I arrive at the Cave at eleven o'clock that night. As I pull into the parking area, I can hear crushed seashells crunching beneath my tires. The one light pole, near the back of the building, is of little value as I try to view the other vehicles. In the shadows, I can see four cars and three pickup trucks. The building appears to be an old whitewashed wood-sided structure. The entrance door, on the side of the building, is ajar, revealing an interior screen door exposed by a yellow bug lamp.

On entering the building, I note six men and four women. All but four are seated at small, round tables. A man and woman are on the left side of the bar, at a pool table. A back door is parallel to the entrance. The stand-only bar sits in front of a backdrop of shelves of wine and whiskey bottles. The counter below the shelves has two sinks and a line of beer-on-tap handles. The lighting is low, except over the pool table, where an illuminated Abita Beer sign hangs overhead. A large floor speaker sits to the right of the back door, bouncing a Led Zeppelin tune off the gray-painted block walls. Two men stand across from the bar, playing a ring-and-nail game. The ring is suspended from the ceiling on a string, and the object is to swing the ring to encircle the nail on the wall. Echoing music, laughter, and small talk fill the bar with a surround sound of nonsense noise.

No one looks up as I enter, except the bartender leaning against the back counter. His eyes follow my entrance. He's a thin-faced man in his early thirties, slender and more than six feet tall. A red skeleton-head decal overpowers his black T-shirt. His dark hair is pulled back into a ponytail. Both arms are laced with tattoos.

"What'd you have?" His accent is pure Cajun.

"Bud."

"Bottle is two fifty. Draft is one fifty. Pick your poison."

"Bottle." I decide to take the safe road, not knowing when the glasses were last cleaned.

Popping the top on the bottle, he continues his questioning. "Ain't seen you before. You either a cop, looking for somebody, or just crazy. Which you be?"

"Not a cop. Looking for Viper. And just half crazy."

The bartender smiles for the first time. "Not here, no. Wanna leave a message?"

"No, I think I'll wait awhile."

"No law against that. Help yourself. Name's Matt if you need anything." Leaning back against the counter, he breaks off eye contact, which tells me he's through with our conversation.

"Justin," I reply. Matt nods and moves to the other end of the bar to help a waiting customer.

Picking a table along the side, I put my back to the wall so I have a clear view of both doors.

After an hour and a couple of beers, nothing changes, except for six more people being added to the present company. Right after midnight, a strange-looking man enters the bar. He's dressed in camo shorts, a dark T-shirt, sandals, and an animal vest. I can see a rope belt tied around his waist. His hair is long and unruly. He has a heavy beard with a streak of white on the left side and one white eyebrow. I guess he's in his late twenties.

The man heads over to the bar, and Matt greets him as someone he knows. After a short conversation, Matt makes a motion toward me, and the man looks around to make eye contact. Smiling gently, he slowly walks over to my table and holds out his hand. A wood crucifix tied to a piece of rope dangles from his neck.

"Around here, they call me John. Welcome to the den of iniquities. I hope you're here as an observer and not a participant."

"Justin Lancer. No, not a participant," I say. John's smile and eye contact are intoxicating. I feel as if I'm meeting an old friend.

"Matthew tells me you are looking for Viper. May I sit, Mr. Lancer?"

"Yes, and call me Justin."

John takes a chair.

I continue in the hope he knows Viper. "You seem to be familiar with Matt. Do you know Viper also?"

"Mr. Lancer, I know all the lost souls of the night. That's my ministry. I'm what you call a ragpicker. Do you know that term?"

"No, can't say I do. But I'm sure you can enlighten me."

"Have you ever heard of a writer by the name of Og Mandino? He's a great storyteller and an author of more than a dozen self-help books. His most famous book is *The Greatest Salesman in the World*. Any of this ring a bell?"

"The title of that book sounds familiar, but I have to admit his name and the story itself escape me."

"You should pick up a copy when you get a chance. I highly recommend any of Mr. Mandino's books."

Our conversation is interrupted as Matt brings a steaming cup of coffee and places it in front of John. "Drink up." It sounds more like an order than a customer delivery.

"Thank you, Matthew," John responds.

Turning to me, Matt asks, "Another Bud?"

"Sure," I reply.

Matt stares back at John before leaving.

"It's none of my business, but I sense a little tension between you two," I say.

"Matthew doesn't like me hanging around. He says I'm not good for his business."

"You mean being a ragpicker?"

"Oh yes, the ragpicker. One of Mr. Mandino's books, *The Greatest Miracle in the World*, has a character named Simon Potter. Simon devotes his life to rescuing people from drugs, crime, broken families, and crushed dreams or just helping them get back on the right path. Souls who are often deemed invisible in today's world. Simon's idea is to renew their strength, courage, and faith through simple techniques and objectives that are repeated day after day. Eventually, the practices are transmitted to our subconscious mind and acted upon. So if we repeat our goals, desires, and objectives daily, positive thoughts replace our negative thoughts. It's truly fascinating how the subconscious mind works."

Matt stops by and leaves me a beer without speaking.

"So, John, the name Simon Potter is to make us relate to Simon Peter of the New Testament, right?"

"Bravo, Mr. Lancer. One of the greatest ragpickers of all time. That's enough about me, Mr. Lancer. What line of work do you do?"

"I'm an investigative reporter for the *New Orleans Chronicle*. I'm doing some background work on a man named Raymond Morone. Does that name mean anything to you?"

"No, I can't say it does. But I take it there must be some relationship between this man and Viper. That is why you're here. Am I correct in assuming that?"

Before I can answer, a group of goth-looking people enter the bar: five men and two women, all dressed in black. Two of the men are wearing three-quarter-length black coats. Their faces are painted with a white makeup that highlights their black lipstick and eyebrows. All of them, both men and women, have black hair that hangs at shoulder length. The leader in the front wears a pair of calf-high black leather military boots. On his neck is a tattoo of a two-headed snake. Walking straight out the back door, they disappear in less than a minute.

"I'm sorry, John. What were you asking?"

"No matter, Mr. Lancer. I believe I have my answer."

"What's out that back door?"

"The den of the Viper. That's where the snakes gather to smoke a little dope, drink, and talk. Not a place you want to visit if you're not a snake. If I can suggest, don't go back there. Tell Matthew you'd like to speak to Viper and have a good reason why he'd leave his den."

Matt fills a tray with seven beers and hurries out the back door. As he reenters the bar area, he swings by our table and picks up John's coffee cup. "John, time for you to get."

John smiles. "Thank you, Matthew. I'll see you soon."

"Yeah, right," replies Matt.

I pull a business card from my pocket and hand it to Matt. "Please ask Viper if he will talk with me for a minute. Tell him Dominic sent me."

Matt looks at my card and heads out the back door again.

"Good luck, Mr. Lancer," John says. "I've been asked to leave, so I will dust off my sandals and return another time."

"How can I get ahold of you?" I ask. "Our conversation never got around to what you know about Viper. I think it may be significant to my investigation."

"I'll be around. You seem to be a nice man, Mr. Lancer. Please take care as you walk around the lost souls of the night. A rope of three cords is not easily broken. Just remember, there is strength in numbers. That works for evil as well as good." John smiles and exits the bar.

Within a minute or two, Matt reenters the seating area and returns to the bar. Not making eye contact with me, he tells me he left my message but received no reply. Now I must wait and see if Viper appears.

At one o'clock in the morning, two of Viper's male companions come through the back door, both with beers in hand. I can't tell from this distance if there is alcohol in the bottles or if they might be used as weapons. One of the men wanders over to the side door and leans on the wall. The other one pulls a chair over to the back door. Both men are unnoticed by the customers inside.

Matt makes eye contact with me and turns his back away from the seating area. I feel my heartbeat pick up pace as I slowly drop my right hand under the table and place it on the handle of my .380.

Viper enters the room, followed by a third man. The third man, in a three-quarter-length black coat, positions himself at the bar, facing the back-wall mirror, giving himself a full view of my table. Matt disappears behind a small white door marked "Men." My index finger moves down to the safety. Viper takes a final look around the bar and proceeds to my table. After pulling out a chair, he sits down. He pulls out my card and flicks it onto the table.

As he stares at me, I can see his yellow contacts with vertical pupils, resembling snake eyes. His face is covered in white makeup. Black outlines circle his mouth and eyebrows. His straight black hair hangs shoulder length.

"You've got five minutes."

"Dominic tells me you know Raymond Morone. I've been talking to him at the prison. Maybe you can help shed some light on his story. He's headed for the state pen if no new information is found. What can you tell me about Raymond?"

Viper holds up his hand with two fingers high in the air. His watchdog at the bar circles around the counter, picks up two beers, drops them off at my table, and returns to his original position. The two other men depart from the seating area and leave out the back door.

Viper pushes a beer toward me and places both hands on the table. His black-painted fingernails blend into the dark-colored wood tabletop. Feeling a little drop in the tension, I place both my hands on the table as an offer of good faith.

Viper opens his beer and takes a drink. "I'll tell you what I told Dominic. I saw Raymond the night that girl was killed. He was at the motel in Metairie. That's all the info I have. I saw him, and I left."

Pushing my old beer aside, I open the new one. "What time was that?"

"Around midnight."

"Can I ask you what you were doing there?"

"No."

"Okay. Where was he when you saw him?"

"Standing outside the front door."

"How did he appear? Nervous? Relaxed? Waiting on someone? Hiding in the shadows? What's your take?"

"No, just standing there. Smoking. Not looking around. Pretty normal."

"You said you recognized him at the front door. Where did you know him from?" I ask.

"Didn't say I knew him. Dominic showed me some pics, and I picked him out," Viper replies.

"Did he meet anyone or speak to anyone while you were there?"

"No. I saw him, and I left. That's all, man."

"Did you notice what he was wearing that night?"

"Clothes, man. Just clothes." Viper downs the rest of his beer and sets the empty bottle on the table. "Anything else?"

"One more question. You were able to ID him from a photo, but you don't remember what he was wearing? You can do better than that."

Viper stares at me and leans back in his chair. I stare back and take a drink of my beer, waiting for his answer.

Viper stands, looks over his shoulder at his companion, and tilts his head toward the back door. The man leaves the counter and heads out of the bar area. "Blue jeans. Black T-shirt. Black ball cap."

"Any markings on the cap or T-shirt?"

"Too dark to see," he answers.

"You must have been pretty close to see his face under a ball cap in the dark."

Viper turns without responding and heads for the back door.

"Thanks for the beer," I say.

Within seconds, Matt returns. The bar looks normal again. After finishing my beer and dropping twenty dollars onto the counter in front of Matt, I leave out the side door.

As I sit in my car in a crowd of pickup trucks and dark-colored vehicles, the view over Lake Pontchartrain is breathtaking. The early morning light has not yet crested the horizon. The moon reflects its crescent face and illuminates the calm, brackish water below. There's no wind to touch the tree leaves silhouetted against the moon's reflection. The picture is still, peaceful, and hypnotizing, almost haunting, with the pale white reflections against grays and blacks.

What a contrast between the two worlds, the one inside the building and the one outside.

I sit in silence as my thoughts draw me back to the campsite where my mom, my dad, and I spent many nights sitting on the old pier. Those nights are lost but never forgotten. At that time in my life, I searched for my vocation and life's meaning, facing the same thoughts everyone goes through—thoughts of life and death, sickness and health, despair and hope, hatred and love. *Which way will my journey take me, and what road will I travel? Whom should I trust, and whom should I fear?* They are age-old questions I still struggle with today. I remember my dad paraphrasing poet Robert Frost's 1920 poem "The Road Not Taken": "The road less traveled is not always easy but is the most rewarding." Taking the road less traveled has always been my goal.

A waterfowl screeches, breaking my train of thought. I smile as I pull away from the parking lot and attempt to discern my conversations with Viper and John.

After five hours of sleep, I arise with two things on my mind. First, I intend to call an LSU friend of mine who works at the coroner's office. I'm hoping he can get me the information on the autopsy and pathology report conducted on the first victim. Second, I need to call Dominic to see if he can get me into the house where Raymond was staying. He might also have information on what evidence, if any, was found there.

At ten thirty, I stop by Dunkin' Donuts off I-10 on Veterans Boulevard and grab a cream cheese bagel and some java. I call the coroner's office; give my name to the switchboard operator; and, after a short wait, reach Eric Nelson.

"Justin, how's it going? Long time no see," Eric says in a happy voice.

"Doing well. Life has been good," I respond.

"And what about you and Kate? Still dating, or are you calling to invite me to your wedding?"

"You're a funny man, Eric. Yes, we're still seeing each other. She has an assignment in Hawaii with *National Geographic*. Same old, same old. She can't get off the road, and I'm too stubborn to traipse around the world following her shirttail. Just not me."

"Hawaii? Man, you have it bad if you can't take some time off for Hawaii. You must have an important assignment yourself. So what's up?"

"I've been handed the Raymond Morone case. You familiar with it?"

"Yes, he was arrested for suspicion of multiple murders in the NOLA area. That is a great assignment. How can I help?"

"I just started on the background information on the first victim, Elizabeth Mary DeBoy. I'm hoping you can fill me in on the autopsy and pathology report."

"Well, you know the files are locked while a criminal investigation is going on, so no can do. But if you would like to stop by around eleven, we can grab a bite of lunch and talk about your wedding plans," Eric says, laughing.

Lunch is a code Eric uses in case his conversation is being taped. Call recording was one of the security measures implemented after some city officials tried to cover up the number of deaths attributed to Katrina and their handling of the situation.

"Sounds great. I'll be there at eleven."

"I'll meet you out front by the walkway next to the parking lot."

"Heading your way."

Heading east on Veterans Boulevard, I pick up I-10 toward New Orleans. Taking the Carrollton Avenue exit, I turn onto Washington Avenue and head east on Earhart Boulevard, toward the coroner's office building. Eric is waiting outside with a huge smile on his face. When he jumps into my car, we exchange "Long time no see" greetings.

"How about some Cajun food? You remember the Cajun seafood restaurant on South Broad Avenue?" Eric asks. "We used to eat there when we were on break at LSU. Seems like a hundred years ago."

"That will be a great place. I haven't been there in years. I always ordered the dressed shrimp po'boy and a frosted mug. I'm all in."

During the short trip to the restaurant, Eric talks about his current position at the coroner's office and how much he likes his job. He has a great relationship with his boss and wants to do everything by the book. The rules forbid giving out information on an ongoing investigation. He says he is willing to tell me what is in the reports but isn't willing to give me any copies or papers that can be traced back as a leak at the office. He is willing to do this if the information is used by me as background information and doesn't show up in the *NOLA Chronicle*. I respect his request and agree that all information will be kept in strict confidence. He also says he assisted at the autopsy and ran the pathology report. After I pull into the gravel and broken-shell parking lot at the restaurant, we shake hands as a sign of trust. I appreciate the gesture. My dad always taught me that a man's promise is his code. It seems that such a simple gesture doesn't carry much impact in the world today.

As we enter the restaurant, the appearance takes me back to our days at LSU.

"Look at this place," Eric says. "It hasn't changed in all these years. Look over there at the back table. There is still a hole in the ceiling tile where you pitched a pen into the ceiling a thousand years ago. I can't believe it. Even the tables look the same. A little worse for wear but the same ones."

We order our sandwiches at the counter and pay a little more than I remember from my LSU days. After taking a seat at the back table, we laugh and talk about how we met and hung out together, often cramming for exams and drinking a pot of coffee to stay awake. We used to write little letters on our arms to jog our memory for the final exam. It was a stressful time but a time I wouldn't trade for the world. It was time well spent. My dad told me, "No matter what you do in life, no one can take away your education." It always amazed me how smart he became as I got older.

As we finish our lunch, Eric begins to talk about the autopsy and pathology report. "You're in for a big bonus."

"How's that?"

"They were shorthanded at the crime lab, and my boss

recommended me to help out. And since the three victims were all similar, I assisted the crime lab on all three murders."

"That is a bonus. For starters, what can you tell me about the first victim?"

"I can tell you there was some evidence on the body. As you probably already know, the victim was strangled. Death was from loss of air to the brain. What you don't know is that the strangulation was achieved with a nylon rope. One like you might buy at Home Depot or Lowe's. There were nylon fibers in the wounds. There was also evidence of a struggle. A couple of broken fingernails. I would conclude that the struggle happened at the same time as the strangulation. I say that because under the fingernails were leather fibers. Not just any leather fibers but those from a heat-resistant glove. One like a welder might use. No sexual assault or drugs in the victim's system. Not much more to tell."

"What about that makes you think the struggle and strangulation happened at the same time?" I ask.

"There was one broken fingernail on each hand. That would be consistent with the victim reaching back to try to remove the rope from around the neck. The leather fibers were under each of the broken nails. The fibers varied slightly from each other. This would indicate two similar but different gloves. There were also bruising and abrasion marks on the victim's left leg, below the knee. The leg abrasion had blue vinyl in the wound. The vinyl was consistent with a steering-wheel cover. It was later confirmed by the crime lab that the victim's blood was on the cover."

"What can you tell me about the rope? Wouldn't any piece of rope from the same roll share the same fiber characteristics? So if a piece of rope from the same roll were found, the fibers would be consistent with the rope used in the murder?"

"Yes, that's correct," Eric says. "Each roll would carry a different batch number from manufacturing. All the rope from each manufacturing batch would match. Depending on the size of the roll, each batch may produce ten to twenty rolls. But each batch would carry its unique fiber characteristic."

"So all I have to do is find matching rope and a pair of welder's gloves, and I have my murderer. That sounds easy." I laugh.

"Bingo." Eric raises his can of Diet Coke and smiles. "I can also tell you that all three murders were done from the same roll of rope. The crossover neck burns of the rope were on the right side of the first two victims' necks. That would be consistent with the murderer being next to the victim and not coming from behind. I would say the murderer was known by the victims and was inside the car when the strangulation took place. The third victim's crossover neck burns were on the left side. There were also hair and bloodstains inside the driver's-side door, at the window channel. The third victim was strangled through the window."

"What about the gloves? Any evidence on the last two victims?"

"Yes. There was a match with victims one and two. Glove fiber under their fingernails had the same fiber characteristics. There was no glove fiber under the nails of the third victim. That's about all the info I have currently. If something else turns up, I'll give you a call."

"Thanks, man. I can't tell you how much I appreciate your time."

Leaving the restaurant, we talk more about our LSU days, and I thank him for the information. When I drop him off at the coroner's office, we plan another meeting after I have time to digest our conversation.

)

After heading into City Park, I pull over by the entrance sign to give Dominic a call. The phone goes to his voice mail, and I leave a message telling him to call me back when he has time.

City Park is a special place for Kate and me. When she is in town, we spend our Sunday afternoons driving through the park and enjoying the beautiful trails and scenery. The entrance sign states that the park is one of the oldest in the country and dates to 1854. The iconic oak trees, with their moss canopies, have stood the test of time. The 1,300 acres of green space include the New Orleans Museum of Art, themed gardens, biking and walking paths, live concerts, golf, fishing and boat rentals, Festival Grounds, Carousel Gardens Amusement Park and its fairy-tale Storyland playground, and the world's largest grove of mature live oak trees. Pulling away from the entrance, I head to our favorite resting spot, CafA. CafA offers a variety of traditional New Orleans foods. Our early morning treats are the beignets and chicory coffee. By afternoon, we are always ready for New Orleans–style jambalaya.

Sitting down under a moss-covered canopy, I lean back and dare to dream. Memories of taking a paddleboat around one of the eleven lagoons brings a smile to my face. It was a time of laughter and dreams that now seems like one of the fairy tales of days gone by. The thought of a City Park wedding floats through my mind, only to be pushed back into a *Cinderella* storybook waiting for the happily-ever-after ending.

As always, my cell phone rings at the worst time. I consider letting the call go to voice mail, but the ID shows it's Dominic, so I put my dreams aside.

"Hi, Detective. I just wanted to update you on my meetings with Viper and the coroner's office."

"Go ahead. I'm on duty today, but I'm pulled over to take a coffee break."

"Viper was pretty much nonresponsive. Didn't tell me much other than what you have already told me. He is obviously covering for himself as to why he was there in the first place and how he recognized Morone in the dark. Did Morone have any drugs in his system or at his house when he was arrested?"

"No, nothing was found. Yeah, I would guess Viper was passing some weed to someone at the motel. But I don't think it was Morone."

"There was another guy at the Cave. Late twenties, five foot seven, and about a hundred and fifty pounds. Heavy beard and a white streak in his hair and eyebrow. Rustic-looking guy. Goes by the name of John."

Dominic lets out a loud laugh. "You mean John the Baptist. Everyone on the street knows JB. What a clown. JB is out to save the world. Some of the street people think he has the gift of prophecy. One of those do-gooders. Real name is Johnathan Mills. Grew up in the

Seventh Ward. Attended Jesuit High School and spent some time in a seminary. Both parents deceased. Works part-time at Café Reconcile on Oretha Castle Haley Boulevard. Strange but harmless."

I let his comments slide by for another day. I found John to be intelligent and sincere, one who really cares about the people on the street. *We could use a lot of Johns in this world*, I think. Changing the subject, I address another matter. "I would like to get a look inside Morone's apartment. Any chance you can get me inside?"

"Sure, I can get you in. He was in an upstairs rental at a house on Esplanade Avenue. I can meet you there in thirty minutes. Address is 2575. Not far off North Broad."

"Yes, I can meet you. The coroner's office also did some work with the crime lab. Do you know if any nylon rope or welder's gloves were found at the apartment or in Morone's work truck? That could tie him to the murders."

"Most of my time was spent at the crime scene and his apartment. There were no tools of any kind found at his apartment. I'll check the investigating report to see what is listed."

"Do you find it strange that a man who works in construction has no tools at his apartment?" I ask.

"No, not really. He apparently worked out of his truck. Did small jobs and picked up material as needed. Only worked for cash."

"Thanks, Detective. I'll see you at the apartment."

As I'm just a few minutes from the address, I take a ride through City Park. Driving alongside the lagoons, I can clearly see the eighteen-hole golf course. Golf carts crossing over the lagoon bridges are a common sight. City Park also has two themed putt-putt courses and a disc golf course that take players through groves of beautiful oak trees. I park for a few minutes and watch as contestants fly their Frisbees across green fairways toward the suspended chain-fashion basket. Pulling out of the park, I follow Esplanade Avenue to the address.

Dominic's car is already there. As we walk up the stairs to the front door, Dominic fills me in on the owners.

"The owners are Mario and Loretta Salvo. They rented to Morone for the last year. No issues with noise or rental payments. Always paid cash. Morone kept to himself, and the Salvos rarely spoke with him. I called ahead, and Mario is expecting us."

I immediately notice that adjacent to the front door of the house are the apartment's outside door and staircase. Yellow police tape stretches across the apartment's front door. Just as Dominic is about to knock on the door, Mario Salvo answers.

"*Buon pomeriggio*, Mario." Dominic greets him in Italian.

"Buon pomeriggio. Welcome, Detective," Mario replies, handing him a key to the apartment. "When you get yellow tape off door? Not good for business."

"Soon, Mario. Soon," Dominic replies.

Mario nods and steps back into his house. "Please hurry. Not good for business."

"I will soon," Dominic says.

Pulling the tape back, Dominic unlocks the apartment door. "The door at the top of the stairs is unlocked. I'll give the key back to Mario. When you are through, just turn the button on the downstairs door lock and replace the tape. I'm headed back to the station to pick up some material. You may look, but nothing leaves the apartment. If you touch anything, it has to go back exactly where it was. If you find anything of interest, call me. You have a pair of gloves?"

"Yes, I have a pair with me. Thanks. I'll send you a text when I leave," I reply. "Was anything removed that I should know about?"

"We bagged empty cans and glasses, along with the trash and toiletries, to check for prints and DNA. You know, the usual stuff. Nothing else. It was pretty clean."

I wait downstairs until Dominic returns the key and pulls away. After ascending the stairs, I find the door at the top is broken in. I'm sure the police broke it to enter. The inside doorframe is broken where a new dead bolt was installed.

Entering the apartment, I put on my pair of gloves and switch on the lights. A single light bulb illuminates the room. The fixture dangles from the ceiling. The stagnant air has a pungent odor like that of a dying animal. The apartment is small. The living room and kitchenette are attached. A short hall leads to the back bedroom and toilet area.

The apartment looks as if a bomb exploded inside. Every drawer is open, with the contents spread out on the floor. Chairs have been turned over in the search for concealed evidence. Three pictures are arranged along the back wall, with their backs facing out. All the backs are solid panels, except for one, whose mounting paper is pulled back. I assess that nothing was in the backing, or the complete picture would have been taken to the crime lab. I count three nail holes in the wall. The number of pictures on the floor agrees. A small TV sits in the corner; its back has been opened. I note spots of fingerprint dusting powder daubed throughout the area.

Rummaging through the material on the floor, I find nothing of importance—a couple of hunting and fishing magazines, with no earmarks, and three empty trash cans. The air-vent covers on the wall have all been removed, as well as the intake air-vent cover. The couch and chair pillows are ripped open and lying on the floor. I can see the underside liners are also torn open. There are two books on the wall shelf, both on astronomy, with no bookmarks or earmarks. Nothing is underlined or noted. In the corner is an older-looking telescope with the initials *RM*. Turning the pictures on the floor around to view them, I note glossy printed pictures of the crescent moon. Two have the crescent on the right side, and one shows it on the left side. I know the pictures are showing the different phases of the moon, but I will need to check them out at the library. I take a picture of them and the books on astronomy with my cell phone for later reference.

The refrigerator and stove are pulled away from the wall, exposing their backs. Opening the refrigerator, I take another picture. Some molded cheese, luncheon meats, bread, a stick of butter, mayo, soda, and beer cans claim most of the inside. There is nothing in the freezer compartment. The stove door is open and contains only a single rack.

The stovetop is off-center and has been lifted off the base. As I lean to look at the back of the stove, I get another jolt of the odor. A dead mouse lies under the spring of a mousetrap.

Continuing down the short hall, I step into the toilet area. It contains a sink, toilet, and shower stall. An incandescent light fixture over the sink hangs by two screws. The toilet tank is open, and the water has been drained. The cabinet door under the sink is open and displays what is left of the toiletries. Towels and washcloths have been pitched into the shower stall. The air-vent cover has been removed and leans against the wall.

Leaving the toilet area, I step into the bedroom and turn on the overhead light. The ceiling fixture has no cover and is hanging, as in the other rooms. All the furniture has been pulled away from the walls. The mattress leans against the side wall. In front of the mattress is a moon poster displaying the phases of the lunar cycle. The two crescent phases are listed as waxing crescent and waning crescent. Waxing, in the first quarter, shows the sickle shape facing to the left, and waning, in the last quarter, shows it facing the right. The four corners of the poster have pinholes that were used for hanging it on the wall. I can see the corresponding holes in the side wall. Clothes and hangers are strewn inside the bed frame. The drawers of the dresser and nightstand are stacked on the floor. The small closet is open and is empty. The air-vent cover has been removed.

I keep thinking I'm missing something. Something Viper said. *Smoking.* He said Morone was standing by the front door, smoking. I walk through the apartment again and find no ashtrays or cigarettes. Viper also said he was wearing a ball cap. Nobody has only one ball cap, yet there are none in his apartment. I take a couple of pictures with my cell phone and send a text to Dominic that I'm leaving. Outside the house, I check the grounds for signs of a smoker. I find nothing. After making some apartment notes, I head to the library.

Browsing through the astrology section at the library, I pick a book on the phases of the moon and one on ancient meanings and symbols. My research on the quarters of the moon reveals that starting with the new moon, each quarter lasts 7.38 days before passing to the next quarter. This gives a cycle time of 29.5 days from new moon to new moon. The moon is directly illuminated by the sun, and the cyclical viewing conditions cause the lunar phases.

Starting with the new moon as phase one, the viewing is divided into eight phases: the new moon, waxing crescent, first quarter, waxing gibbous, full moon, waning gibbous, third quarter, and waning crescent.

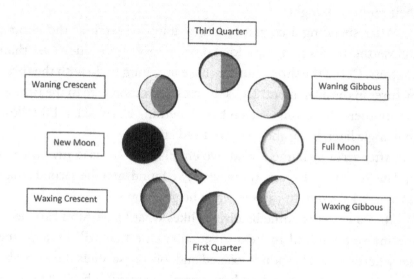

Moon Phases

Waxing means to increase or get bigger. *Waning* means to decrease or get smaller. *Gibbous* refers to a shape that is less than the full circle of a full moon but larger than the semicircle shape of the third-quarter moon. The word *gibbous* comes from a root word that means "humpbacked."

Looking into the ancient meanings and symbols of the moon, I find that the moon is often given a gender. Most of the information dates to the Native Americans and African tribes. The moon, as a feminine symbol, represents rhythm of time, immortality, purity, enlightenment, or the dark side of nature. There are numerous goddesses in mythology who feature the crescent moon, which conveys fertility, secret wisdom, and hidden powers. Artemis and Hecate from Greek mythology and Cerridwen from Celtic mythology date back to early times.

Men are also depicted as lunar deities of the crescent moon, possessing power, influence, and the dark side. The crescent tattoo has a wide array of meanings, indicating magic, mystique, purity, shadow, and even dreams. The tattoo is often paired with one of many wild beasts, such as the bull, cat, owl, wolf, and lion and those who do their hunting at night.

After spending a couple of hours doing research at the library, I close the books and start for home. I have more questions than answers. Could the three murders have anything to do with the three pictures in the apartment? Does the crescent moon date to the time of the murders? It's a long stretch but something to consider. I'll follow that angle later, but right now, I'm tired and hungry.

After arriving home, I send two emails out. One is to my office to update Rocco and let him know what I've found, and the second email is to Eric. I ask him to call me when he gets home.

Rocco answers immediately. He likes what I have found and feels the information will make a great story line that will fit with the daily horoscope. He sounds excited and, of course, ends the email by telling me to get busy and get him something to publish. That's not on my immediate list of things to accomplish, but his ideas don't always reflect mine.

At six thirty, I get a call from Eric. He says he's home and open to talk. I ask if he remembers if the victims had any astrological tattoos. He responds that they did have several tattoos, but he can't remember what they were. He'll check in the morning. We agree to meet for lunch at Cane's Chicken on South Carrollton Avenue at eleven thirty. He'll have the information at that time.

My next task is to put together a time line and apply the moon phases. If there's a connection, a spreadsheet will be valuable in my analysis.

After several hours of work, I drag myself to bed and set the information aside until tomorrow.

CHAPTER 3

Drinking my morning coffee, I mull over my notes from last night. Checking the lunar phases for January, February, and March, I find something interesting. In the month of January, there were two full moons: one on January 1 and another on January 31. A full moon that rises twice in a month is called a blue moon. In February, there was no full moon. March also had two full moons: one on March 1 and another on March 31.

Moon Phases 2018 (America) Central Standard Time

	January	February	March
Full Moon	1st & 31st	none	1st & 31st
Waning Crescent	11-14th	9-13th	11-15th
% Visible	26,18,12,6	33,25,17,11,6	32,24,16,10,5
New Moon	16th	15th	17th
Waxing Crescent	19-22nd	17-21st	19-22nd
% Visible	6,11,18,26	3,7,13,21,31	5,10,18,27,38

Moon Dates

Checking the dates of the three victims' deaths, I find the murders occurred on January 31, February 11, and March 13, the blue moon in January and the waning crescent moon in February and March. It's interesting but no home run. The range of the waning crescent's being five days of the moon's twenty-nine-day cycle in February and March could be a coincidence. The full moon or blue moon is no surprise. It's been documented that there's more criminal activity during a full moon. If there's a pattern here, the blue moon could have been the start of the serial murders, followed by the two crescent-moon phases. I'm sure from this I can spin an interesting story for the *NOLA Chronicle* that will keep Rocco happy. To extend the article's information, I decide to find an astrological seer in NOLA and get my fortune told.

Searching the internet, I come across a list of astrological psychics in the area. I'm hoping to find a blog on which I can read customers' comments and get some feedback on their experiences and a blog that will give me comments on psychics not listed on the internet. These are the ones I'm looking for. After a few minutes of searching, I find a blog called "Haunted New Orleans." There are twenty entries on a clairvoyant who lives in a cabin in a swampy area of the Old Pearl River in Slidell. As always, there are both positive and negative comments on Sister Moon's telepathic abilities, but there are far more positive than negative. Three of the negative comments state that the voodoo woman would not let them enter her house and told them to leave. Another comment says this seer is a descendant of Marie Laveau, New Orleans's queen of voodoo.

I haven't been to this area of the Pearl River in years. I remember taking a private swamp tour with my dad years ago. I must have been ten or eleven. I'll never forget the old wooden stick houses that lined the riverfront, surrounded by moss-covered cypress trees. I still can see the images of swamp people sitting on an extended back porch hanging over the muddy-colored river water. The looks on their ruddy faces and their unwelcoming posture are entrenched in my mind. One was a shirtless man. His brown skin was broken and weather-beaten. White rubber shrimp boots covered the bottom part of his faded blue jeans. I remember the wake of the boat thrashing against the wood pillars that supported his lean-to shack. His never-blinking stare penetrated me with a look that was deep and threatening, one that let me know I had invaded his privacy and home sanctuary. The vison was terrifying, and I had to turn away. The tour guide said that area was known for the practice of voodoo and night hauntings of the ghost of Marie Laveau.

Even today, the name of Marie Laveau is synonymous with New Orleans voodoo. She was a dedicated practitioner of voodoo and dealt in spells, charms, magical items, and curative roots. She is the source of hundreds of tales of horror and spiritual cures in New Orleans.

Digging a little deeper, I pull up a biography on Marie Catherine Laveau. She was born on September 10, 1801, a free Louisiana Creole, in the French Quarter of New Orleans. In 1819, she married a free black man by the name of Jacques Paris, who died in 1820. Marie and Jacques had two daughters who survived into adulthood. She then took on a domestic partner by the name of Christophe Glapion, a white man of French descent. According to birth and baptismal records, they had seven children. Marie died in New Orleans in 1881, at the age of seventy-nine. It is generally believed she's buried in the confines of St. Louis Cemetery No. 1. Due to continued vandalism and destruction of tombs, there's no longer public access to St. Louis Cemetery No. 1. The new rules of the Catholic Archdiocese of New Orleans require you to join an organized tour if you don't have a family member interred there. Considering the information on Sister Moon and Marie Laveau, this is the perfect place for me to start. I decide to try to find Sister Moon this afternoon or at least locate her cabin.

After organizing my notes of the week and starting an article to send to Rocco, I head to Cane's Chicken.

When I arrive, Eric is already inside and has a table in the back of the restaurant. He holds up his cup of soda, and I see he has already received his food and is waiting on me. I order a spicy chicken box combo, pay up, and take my seat. After the normal greetings, Eric starts to tell me about the victims.

"If you were looking for tattoos, you hit a gold mine. Victim one has fourteen, victim two has ten, and victim three has fifteen. Everything from *A* to *Z*."

"What I'm most interested in is anything astronomical. I'm trying to see if maybe the victims had something in common."

Eric pulls out a list and reads me some of the items. "Victim one has several: a lion, which could represent the constellation Leo; a crescent moon; and a shooting star. The moon and star are recent. Victim two has a ring of stars with a heart, a horoscope plate, and a crescent moon. Victim three has a full moon, a heart, and a crescent moon. The heart and crescent moon are new. I'd say within the last several months."

"How can you tell the age?"

"It's just an educated guess, but the brightness of the ink and the sharpness of the edges will indicate a recent inking. Over time, the colors fade, and the edges leak into the surrounding skin."

"Do you see a lot of these types of tattoos?"

"These're quite common. Probably every tattoo parlor in NOLA has a book of astrological tats. Around the French Quarter alone, there are probably two dozen parlors. You might see if any of them specialize in this type, but I have my doubts. I even looked up the number of people with tattoos on Google. I was amazed. Thirty-six percent of Americans between the ages of eighteen and twenty-nine have at least one tattoo. Of those who have tattoos, seventy percent have more than one, and twenty percent have more than five. Seventy-two percent of adults have tattoos usually hidden by clothing."

"Thanks. I could be running into a dead end, but at least they have this in common. What I find interesting is that Morone has pictures of different moon phases and astronomical books in his apartment. The dots might connect, or maybe it's just another case for the chaos theory. I think I'll run down to the French Quarter and look around."

"Good luck. If you need any more information, give me a call."

We finish our lunch, and Eric heads back to work. I hang out for a few more minutes and pick out some of the tattoo parlors on my phone before heading to the French Quarter. After parking on Decatur Street, near Café Du Monde, I walk past the St. Louis Cathedral toward the New Orleans Historic Voodoo Museum.

The streets are jammed with tourists. Barkers stand outside restaurant doors, passing out discount coupons and enticing prospective customers to step inside. The first two parlors I stop in don't impress me. They contain mostly tourists' T-shirts and New Orleans souvenirs, with a rack or two of dirty magazines and some smoking apparatuses. A single tattoo artist sits in his reclining chair, waiting for his next customer. Not much to look at. My next parlor is named Vaping and Tattoos. Entering the parlor, I see that most of the storefront is set up for e-cigarette customers, with a small back room for tattoos. Three-ring notebooks are spread along the counter with tattoo samples. On the wall over the counter are more tattoo illustrations, with photos of happy-appearing customers. Nothing on the wall jumps out at me. The notebooks on the counter are arranged by subject. I page through the small astrological binder and make note of a dozen or so moon phases.

"Wat cha need, my man? Two for one today. Pic you one; next one is free. Or bring your lady back, and we ink her real sexy-like. Wat cha say?"

As I look at the young man, it takes me a minute to respond. His bald head is covered in a spiderweb tattoo. A black widow hanging by a thread accents his cheek. Both arms are colored to his fingertips.

"Not today. Just stopped in to see what you have. I do have a question."

"Answers free today too."

"Does your artist do custom work or just what you have in the notebooks?"

The young man looks around to see if anyone can hear him, and he leans into the counter. "You go see my cuz Andre. He best in town. Rampart Street, past the Voodoo Temple. Tell him you from Willy."

"Thanks, Willy. I'll do that."

Willy winks and slides off to another customer.

Leaving the store, I head to North Rampart Street and turn right toward the Voodoo Spiritual Temple. As I approach the temple, a crowd of people are exiting the front door. Looking into the storefront window, I read their mission statement:

> The Voodoo Spiritual Temple and Cultural Center's mission is to provide service that meets the needs of all mankind, which allows him or her to fulfill their quest in the divine plan of the universe. The temple was established in 1990 by Priestess Miriam Chamani and her husband, Priest Oswan Chamani. It is the only formally established spiritual temple with a focus on traditional West African spiritual and herbal healing practices currently existing in New Orleans. It has been serving New Orleans natives and visitors of all nationalities for twenty-seven years.

From my vantage point, I see the Carnal Ink overhead sign a couple of buildings down. Inside the parlor, all the walls are covered with photos and artist renderings. Chairs and tables line both side walls. Six artists are busy at work as their electric needles give off a low-pitched buzzing sound. Conversation is high, with an occasional moan or curse word interjected. Illustration books line the counter and two tables. Four standing customers are either waiting their turn or just browsing until they get up enough nerve to make the decision.

As I scan one of the larger books marked "Astrological," a man from behind the counter approaches me. He looks to be in his fifties, with a potbelly, shoulder-length white hair, and chopper sideburns. An American flag is tattooed on his right arm, and a Marine bulldog is on his left.

"Interested in the astrological tattoos? We have several artists who can help you with that. We have some of the best artists in NOLA."

"Well, yes and no. I'm looking for the artist Andre. He comes highly recommended."

"Andre isn't here anymore, but we have artists who are exceptionally good. If you want to set up an appointment, I can handle that. My name is Jim Carnes. I'm the owner here."

"Thanks, Jim. I'm Justin Lancer." Handing him a business card, I continue. "I'm doing an article for the *New Orleans Chronicle* on tattoo parlors and was just checking out some of them in the Quarter."

"I'm your man for that. Look around, and I'll get you a business brochure," he responds.

"The pictures on the wall of the crescent moon—did Andre do those, by any chance?"

"Yeah, I hated to lose him. He was one of the best custom designers I'd ever seen. Astrological stuff was his specialty. Real talent that boy had. That split-face wolf to the right—that's one of his. He called it the creature of the night."

"Do you know when that was designed?"

"About three or four months ago."

"You wouldn't happen to know who it was designed for, would you?"

"No, can't say I do. Andre would know. We don't keep records by name. Only cash transactions. Our range of customers aren't exactly what you would call model citizens, if you know what I mean. Don't get me wrong; we get some high social people here too, but the scale leans way left."

I pull up Morone's picture on my phone and show it to Jim. "Do you recognize this person?"

"He kind of looks familiar, but we get a lot of people in here. Can't say for sure."

"Any idea where Andre might have gone?"

"No, can't say I do. He just came in one day, packed up his tools, and left. Never gave a reason; just left. I actually owe him a day's pay." Jim looks around the store as a group of four enter his store. "Take a look around, and I'll get you a brochure."

Jim steps into the back, and I seize the opportunity to take a picture of the wolf design. The design depicts a wolf with light-colored hair on one half of its face, with a yellow eye, and a dark and sinister black-haired face on the other side, with a red eye. It's an amazing visual of good and evil.

Two-Faced Wolf

When Jim returns, he hands me a brochure. "Who did you say recommended Andre?"

"Guy named Willy. Works at another parlor in the Quarter."

"Oh, him. I'm not saying anything bad about Willy, but that's one kid I was glad to get rid of. Couldn't depend on him. One day he went to get us some lunch and never returned. Just took my twenty bucks and left. Never saw him again. Probably the best twenty bucks I ever spent."

"Would you mind sharing Andre's address you have on file?"

"Sorry, can't do that. Wouldn't matter though; he moved several times while he worked here. I only update all that info when I have to file with Uncle Sam. Too hard to keep track of these people daily."

"Could you give me a last name?"

"LeBlanc. Andre LeBlanc."

"Thanks, Jim. I'll look over the brochure, and if I have any more questions, I'll give you a call."

"Let me see that picture again." Jim calls over one of the other artists. "Nate, you ever seen this guy in here?"

"Yeah, he's been in here several times. Always dealt with Andre. Had a chick with him one time. Think she got inked."

"Do you know where I can find Andre? It's important," I say.

"No, man. Andre was a loner. Kept to himself. Didn't have many friends."

"Thanks, Nate," Jim responds. Nate returns to his table.

"Jim, did Andre hang out with anyone here that you know of?"

"No, these guys are in competition with each other. Each one is trying to crush the other guy. Makes it tough to keep artists, but it also pushes them to show out. Egos are high."

"Do you keep an appointment book?" I ask.

"Most of these guys keep their own book. Every now and then, I write one down and give it to one of the guys who isn't busy, but they pretty much handle their own."

"Thanks, Jim. I appreciate your help."

"No problem. Number is on the brochure. When you need to schedule your appointment, call me."

After leaving Carnal Ink, I swing back by Vaping and Tattoos. Maybe Willy knows more than he is letting on. As I approach the front of the store, Willy is outside puffing on an e-cigarette.

"Willy, Andre is no longer at the Carnal Ink. Do you know how I can get a hold of him?" I ask.

Without answering, Willy pulls out his cell phone, selects a number, and pushes his call button. A recording comes on: "The number you have reached either is disconnected or is no longer in service."

"Nope. Know nothing. Jut ask around. Can't help ya."

Handing him one of my cards, I say, "If you find out anything, give me a call. I'll make it worth your while."

"Sure." Willy turns away and reenters the parlor.

Leaving the French Quarter at three fifteen, I pick up US-190 East and turn right onto Highway 1090. Passing over I-10, I turn right onto the I-10 service road and follow it till it ends at the Pearl River. Off to the left is a dirt road with a wooden sign: Old Pearl River Road. After about a half mile, I see some signs of inhabitants along the riverside. The deeper I go, the swampier the landscape becomes. After another eight minutes, I find myself in another world. Dragonflies hover over the flat, grassy terrain as the wind breathes life into the tall grass. A large grasshopper lands on my windshield and takes flight after peering through the clear glass. A small feral pig crosses the road in front of me only to disappear in the adjacent field.

Wood river shacks appear along the river's edge. Red reflectors nailed to weathered half-painted fence posts mark property lines. An occasional rock garden or family grave site can be seen on the property lot. Hand-painted No Trespassing signs clutter the area. Most of the shacks are made of wood, with fading or chipping paint and tin roofs. Chairs and other household goods sit on the sun-shaded front porch. Uncut grass, old trucks, and rusted machine parts litter most of the yards. Fishing boats and pirogues are common; their noses are raised off the ground by concrete blocks. Hanging gray-colored moss dangles like Christmas tinsel from every tree. The tinsel floats gently in the breeze like an inviting hand beckoning me to step closer. A cur appears from underneath a wood porch, shouting to his owner of an intruder.

Within a short distance, I can see a blue-painted house. A shingle is nailed to a wood post, announcing the whereabouts of Sister Moon. Pulling over the covered culvert, I park on a grass-worn flat. A middle-aged black man is working in a small garden off the left of the house. He stops his work and leans on his hoe handle to face me. An elderly dark-skinned woman sits on the porch. She wears a light blue dress, with a black turban wrapped around her head. A cat arches its back as it stands up from her lap. Another cat sits on the edge of the bottom step but makes no notice of my arrival. After exiting my car, I stop at the bottom step to be respectful of her space and privacy.

Before I can speak, she sets the cat on the porch and addresses me. "You seek someone, yes?"

"Yes, I'm looking for someone who might be involved—"

Sister Moon holds up her hand to stop my explanation. "But you are no police, no, but are seeking someone of great importance, yes?"

"Yes, that is true."

"Step closer so I may see you. My old eyes need to look into you, yes."

As I step onto the porch, both cats dash off and quickly disappear around the side of the house. Leaning forward in her rocking chair, Sister Moon continues. "You seek an evil man, yes? But why do you seek evil? This is not good for you, no."

"What I seek is justice for those involved."

Sister Moon leans back in her chair and laughs. "You speak of justice. Justice like for my people or your people? Justice should be same, yes?"

"Yes, it should be, but it isn't always the same. We all carry our own prejudices. The way we are raised or where we live. Our education or the people we associate with. Everything from the clothes we wear to the way we look affect how we're judged. We're doing better, but we may never get to where we look at a person and don't see his coverings. Not in my lifetime anyway."

"You speak true, yes." She motions for the man in the garden to continue his work. "Come inside, and I will tell you about the person you seek."

Sister Moon stands and pushes open the screen door. As I enter behind her, another cat jumps from the top of a cluttered chest and runs into the back room. An oscillating fan sits on a corner table and pushes a musty odor around the room. To the right is a black potbellied wood heater with tin ductwork that turns at a right angle and exits out the side wall. A chest and pie cupboard line the opposite wall. The back wall is lined with several tables covered in every imaginable voodoo artifact and statue. Herbs hang from nails on the wall. Small soil pots with different types of plants line the side wall. A back-room doorframe is draped with a multicolored curtain. Hanging next to the doorframe is a picture of Marie Laveau. In the middle of the room is a round wood table. Sister Moon motions for me to sit.

Extending her hands over another table, she chants some incomprehensible words, and then she picks up one of several decks of cards and joins me at the table. "It is twenty dollars for reading. More if you are satisfied."

She stares at me for a few moments, and I realize she wants the money up front. After I pay her, she smiles, places the deck in front of me, and starts the reading.

"Cut into three stacks, yes."

I do as I'm told.

After turning over the top card of each stack, she stops. "These are the cards of your journey."

Looking down, I see that the deck she has chosen is of astrological symbols. The first three cards are star constellations.

"You are Taurus, yes?" she says.

I have to think for a minute to remember my zodiac sign. "Yes, I was born under Taurus, the bull."

She turns three more cards and looks at me but doesn't comment. The next six cards get the same response. Pushing all the upturned cards aside, she says, "These are not part of your journey, no."

In the next three cards, a full moon appears. She touches this card, hesitates for a moment, and moves it away from the other two cards. "The person you seek is a man. A creature of the night."

So far, she hasn't told me much I don't already know.

When she turns the next three cards, a crescent moon appears. She again hesitates and then removes this card and places it in alignment with the full moon. "This sign is of importance. The one you seek is beneath the crescent moon."

"But what does that—"

Sister Moon holds up her hand again to interrupt me. She slowly turns three more cards. A black scythe is in the group. Removing this card, she places it with the other two. She looks at me in a queer way. "The one you seek is not here. You are mistaken in your search."

"What do you mean he's not here? How can he not be here?"

"The one you seek is not among the living but sleeps beneath the crescent moon."

"I don't understand. What does that mean?"

"Look to the dead, not the living." Picking up her cards, she stands as a signal that our reading is over.

Confused, I don't even know what to ask her.

Sister Moon adds to my confusion with her parting words. "We will meet again about the one you seek. Take heed. Those in your search are not who they seem, no. I give you gris-gris to carry with you. Do not go into the night without this protection. You are dealing with the creatures of the dead."

She picks up a small leather bag, hands it to me, and walks into the back room. Standing in the front room by myself, I can't help but think, *What the hell just happened?* Looking down at the drawstring bag, I stick it in my pocket. I'm not sure what this is right now, but as soon as I can get a signal on my phone, I intend to find out. After leaving another ten dollars on the table for the extra protection, as if I believe all she told me, I leave the house.

Once I get back to US-190, I pull over at a convenience store and check my phone for a signal. With two bars, I google *gris-gris*: "A gris-gris is a two-inch by three-inch drawstring bag made of red flannel, chamois, or leather. Special herbs, stones, personal effects, hair, fingernails, roots, bones, coins, charms, or crystals are placed inside the bag for an intended use by a voodoo priest or priestess."

Not sure what I'm carrying around, I place the bag in the glove compartment. Thinking Dominic might be able to help me find some information on Andre, I leave a message for him to please call me. I step inside the convenience store and pick up a soda. When I get back to my car, the phone rings.

"What's up?" Dominic asks.

"Could you do me a favor and check on a guy by the name of Andre LeBlanc? He's a tattoo artist and was working in the French Quarter at a place named Carnal Ink. He specializes in astrological signs and designs. He seems to have disappeared around the same time Morone was arrested."

"And how does this have anything to do with Morone?" Dominic asks.

"Well, all three victims had this type of tattoo, and along with the pictures and books that were in Morone's apartment, maybe there is some relationship."

Dominic is silent for a few seconds before he turns a buzz saw on me. "I'm not here to help you play detective. That's for those who have earned the title. I was told you were going to do a story on the Morone case and the murders. That's all. What kind of crap is this? You sound like you're trying to reopen this case. Are you trying to get this bum back on the street? This case is closed as far as I'm concerned. We have a witness, fingerprints that match a victim in Morone's truck, and DNA at his apartment. So cut the crap and get back to doing your job, and I'll do mine."

I feel my face flush, and I fail miserably in trying to remain calm. "Your witness is a flake. And just because you have prints and DNA, that doesn't make him a murderer until you have credible evidence and a motive. That is up to a jury to decide. What has happened to innocence till proven guilty? So the guy was having a fling with a couple of girls who ended up dead. This guy Andre might also have had contact with the victims. And about Viper—his story is so inconsistent it stinks. There're a lot of loose ends here. I *am* doing my job, and you should—"

Dominic hangs up on me. By now, I'm steaming. *What a jerk.* I sit in my car as my heart races. At least I got some new information about the fingerprints and DNA. My next move is to call Rocco to let him know what's going on, but I need to relax for a minute and get my thoughts in order. The past several hours have given me a brain overload. I decide to stop by Café Du Monde to unwind.

Before I reach my next destination, I get a call from Rocco, one I am expecting. To my surprise, he's laughing.

"What the hell are you doing out there?" Rocco tries to sound intense but can't maintain the charade. "You got Dominic crying like a baby. You really got his goat." He laughs. "And you know what? I'm loving it."

"The guy just went off like a cannon. Says I'm interfering with a closed case. A man is sitting in jail, waiting for his trial. The only thing closed is Dominic."

"He's pissed. Said you're questioning his investigation. Don't worry about him; I'll handle him. You just keep doing whatever you're doing. Keep stirring the pot. I think you inspired him to dig a little deeper.

That's a good thing. He's overwhelmed with work. Give him some space. He'll come back around. In the meantime, I'll handle him."

"Okay, and thanks."

"Now, get off your butt, and get me something to print, or I'll add to your burden."

"I've got some great background information. You'll be impressed."

"Impress me later. Right now, I have a paper to run. I need print. Get to work." The phone goes dead.

That's the Rocco I'm used to. I have to smile.

After driving back to NOLA, I find a parking spot by the St. Louis Cathedral and walk toward the river, to Café Du Monde. Finding a small two-seat table on the patio, I order a chicory coffee and some beignets. The street is beginning to fill with evening tourists, and peddlers line the sidewalk in front of Jackson Square along Decatur Street. A couple of horse-and-buggy rides hug the curb, waiting for their next customer. A caricature artist sets up her chair and easel. An Uber driver stops in front of the café and drops off a young couple.

Sipping my coffee, I think about whom I can contact to follow up on Andre LeBlanc. I don't think I'm going to get much help from Dominic. I could push Willy some more and maybe find out Andre's last known address. My gut tells me there is more to Andre than just a tattoo artist. Somehow, I've got to see if there's any police information on him. And what about the strange reading from Sister Moon? I must file that away for another time. Right now, the message makes no sense.

My thoughts are interrupted by a familiar voice.

"Good evening, Mr. Lancer. Are you waiting on someone?" Johnathan Mills, a.k.a. John the Baptist, is standing to the side of my table. He's holding a cup of steaming coffee in one hand and what appears to be a tattered Bible held together with a wide rubber band in the other. His friendly smile captures me instantly.

"No, John. Please sit down. I was just unwinding."

"If you would rather be alone in your thoughts, I understand. I find great peace when I set aside the pressures around me and just let my mind wander about."

"Please, join me. As a matter of fact, you may be able to help me."

As he takes the other chair, I notice John eyeing the last two beignets on my paper plate, and I push the powder-covered pastries toward him. "May I offer you a beignet? I've already had my limit."

"Indeed, you may." John smiles. Within seconds, his unruly beard is covered in powdered sugar. Using one of the napkins on the table, he does the best he can to wipe away the evidence. "Messy but well worth the effort." The last one disappears with a similar result. "I have always wondered how many of these puffed delights I could eat." John laughs. "I have to tell a story on myself. When I was in school, a group of us came here. I was boasting that I could eat a hundred beignets. When the group dared me and pooled their money, the bet was on. I never reached my goal of a hundred, because we ran out of money at eighty. Those guys were really mad, but they never challenged me again."

As we toast with our coffee cups, John continues. "Enough about me. How may I be able to help you?"

"I'm trying to find a man by the name of Andre LeBlanc. He's a tattoo artist and was working at Carnal Ink on North Rampart Street."

"I know of the store. It's over by the Voodoo Spiritual Temple. I have to say, Mr. Lancer, your work certainly brings you to some very unusual places."

"So you're familiar with the store?"

"No, I wouldn't go that far. I'm familiar with the Voodoo Temple. Contrary to most opinions, voodoo is still practiced in this area and has quite a following. Rituals and voodoo spiritualism remain entrenched in some of the cultures around New Orleans. Most people believe that voodoo is only practiced by those of African, Haitian Creole, or Dominican descent. That may have been true when it first appeared, but it's not true anymore. No, Mr. Lancer, voodoo here is alive and well."

"I know. I had firsthand experience with a priestess by the name of Sister Moon."

"Mr. Lancer, don't take Sister Moon lightly. There are many stories of her spells and power among believers. A receptive mind can be dangerous. If your work is taking you along this path, I strongly advise you not to proceed."

"I agree. It was a onetime meeting for some background information on an article I'm writing. I have no intention of going back."

"Mr. Lancer, may I ask you a personal question?"

"Sure, John. Ask me anything."

"Do you pray?"

The question stuns me, and I hesitate with my answer. "I would have to say, not like I used to. I grew up in a Catholic family. Both parents took interest in seeing that I was exposed to the doctrines of the church and educated in a Catholic school. As I got older and started college, I slipped away from the church and became a little more secular in my thoughts."

"Yes, that is a dilemma of a lot of colleges and universities. The move from God-reliance to self-reliance is a real issue that is growing in our midst." After removing the rubber band from his Bible, he flips through until he finds a particular holy card. Handing me the card, he continues. "I'm sure with your background, you remember Saint Michael the archangel. There is a simple prayer on the back. The last few lines ask that through the power of God, Satan be cast into hell, along with all the evil spirits that roam the world seeking the ruin of souls. It's a prayer of protection. I would like for you to have it."

"Thank you, John. I will keep it with me. I must really be in need." I laugh. "This is the second item of protection I've received today."

John has a questioning look on his face.

"I received a gris-gris bag from Sister Moon. She told me it was for my protection against the dead."

John reaches over and touches my hand. "Mr. Lancer, please listen to me. A gift from a priestess of voodoo has ramifications. Do you still have this item?"

"Yes, it's in my car."

"The mere possession of such an item is acceptance. It's quite different from buying a souvenir. Accepting an item from a priestess ties the two of you together. You must destroy this item. It can't just be thrown out but must be burned in fire. And please do it tonight before you sleep."

John seems adamant about the item, and I must admit his words scare the hell out of me.

"I had no idea. I'll do as you say."

John leans back in his chair and gives a sigh of relief. "Thank you. We can never be too careful when dealing with voodoo spiritualism. Their service is with Satan. When Jesus was tempted by the devil in the desert, Matthew 4:10 gives us Jesus's words of rebuke: 'Away with you, Satan! Scripture has it: You shall do homage to the Lord your God; him alone shall you adore.'"

I sit in silence for a few minutes, turning the holy card around in my hands. John breaks the tension.

"Since I have rocked your foundation," he says, smiling, "do you have any more information on this man Andre LeBlanc?"

"No, just a name and occupation. He has a cousin at another parlor in the French Quarter. Young guy by the name of Willy at the Vaping and Tattoos shop. Willy was the one who gave me his name. That's about where the lead ended. I was going to see if Andre had a prior record, but I think I lost my contact with the police."

"Well, I'm your man. I can assure you that if Andre is on the street, I will find him. As for a police report, I do have some friends in high places. I'll see what I can do."

"Yes, I believe you do." I laugh.

"Believe I do what?" John asks.

"Believe you have friends in high places," I joke, holding up the holy card.

John strokes his beard as a smile covers his whole face. "I'll consider that a compliment, Mr. Lancer. I'll ask around and let you know what I find."

"I can't thank you enough. How can I get in touch with you?"

"You can usually find me at Café Reconcile most days, helping out with lunch. It's a wonderful nonprofit youth ministry. It helps at-risk youth develop needed job training. Food is great. You should check it out."

"I will. Thanks. Well, I need to get home and get an article to my boss before he fires me. It was good talking with you, and thanks for the advice."

"You're very welcome, Mr. Lancer. And please don't forget what I told you about that little item you have."

"I will take care of that when I get home. Thanks again. And maybe when all this is over, we'll have to revisit this question of beignets. This one is on me."

John gives a big grin and shakes my hand. "Indeed, we will."

After throwing a tip onto the table, I leave the café and drive home. My mind is spinning in a hundred different directions. After I arrive home, I remember the gris-gris bag in the glove compartment. Upon retrieving it, I head directly to my backyard. After placing the item in a small metal bowl, I douse it with charcoal starter fluid and set it on fire. Remembering the holy card, I remove it from my pocket, turn it over, and read the short prayer.

I watch as the fire fades and the last of the ashes turn cold. Feeling better about the day, I enter the house to finish my article for Rocco. Tomorrow I will search again for Andre and get ready to meet with Morone.

CHAPTER 4

"Good morning, Detective DeAngelis. You're here bright and early," the receptionist says as I enter the department's office.

"Couldn't sleep. Figured I'd catch up on some work."

"Fresh coffee in the break room," she responds.

Taking a seat at my desk, I start my computer and drum a pencil on my desktop. The more I think about my conversations with Justin and Rocco, the more agitated I become. I force myself to pull up the information on Morone from my computer's closed filings. Procrastinating, I wander over to the break room, hoping someone might be there to start a conversation. With no rescuers in sight, I pour a cup of coffee and take a seat. Through the break room's glass wall, I watch as my computer screen slowly fades to black as it sets itself into sleep mode.

As I'm a detective, the what-if question conquers my ego. Stopping by the file room, I pull all the paperwork on Raymond Lester Morone. Back at my desk, I meticulously read through the paperwork and compare it to the information entered in my computer.

"Okay, so Viper isn't a great witness," I say out loud.

"Did you say something?" the receptionist asks.

"No, just talking to myself."

"This place will do that to you." She laughs.

Reading over the information for a second time, I convince myself the fingerprints and DNA sample of a victim might be enough to get most of a jury to swing a guilty verdict. But I also agree with Justin that if I could find a more credible witness, it could be a slam dunk. I'm still puzzled that Morone has no information verifying who he is and where he comes from. There should be a paper trail on a man who has lived for thirty-seven years. The only answer is that the name he's using isn't his real name.

Digging deeper, I'm able to access the sheriff's office's files pertaining to his arrest, incarceration, and body search. The body search is a normal procedure that identifies any birthmarks or physical abnormalities unique to the person. The inspection notes an appendix scar, a scar from surgery on his left shoulder, and tattoos on his chest. One tattoo jumps out at me. It depicts a split-faced wolf with one yellow and one red eye. On either side is a crescent moon encircled by stars.

I immediately do a search on the tattoo artist Andre LeBlanc. In less than a minute, I get a hit. Andre Demonte LeBlanc has five prior arrests: two for assault, one for possession of drugs, one for possession of stolen goods, and one for DUI. He is currently on probation but failed to check in last month to his parole officer. He has a current warrant issued for failure to appear.

Pulling up his profile, I see that LeBlanc is twenty-eight, five foot eight, and 160 pounds. He has dark brown skin and claims to be French. He has a black crew cut and small goatee. Both arms and neck are covered in tattoos. He has a large scar over his right eyebrow. I make note of his parole officer and last known address. In the files, I find a list of stolen goods confiscated from Andre at the time of his arrest. The items were stolen from Beesly Hardware Store in Mandeville in December 2017. The two break-in thieves were arrested on January 30, 2018, and later identified Andre LeBlanc as a person they traded merchandise with in exchange for tattoo services. Since the two arrested were serving time on the dates of two of the murders, I exclude them from my suspect list. That leaves Andre as a person of interest in this case.

Running down Andre's possession list, I see the items include small electric tools, saw blades, hand tools, welder face shields, and two rolls of nylon rope. I quickly reference the items' numbers and find the items are still in the evidence property room, awaiting release. Checking the Beesly Hardware Store inventory of stolen items, I see that several items are not listed in Andre's possession. They include a box of Case pocketknives, a registered handgun, and a third roll of nylon rope. I'm short a roll of rope. I call the property room to verify that the two rolls of nylon rope confiscated during Andre's arrest are still present.

"Property room. Sergeant Beckum."

"Hey, Larry. Dominic DeAngelis."

"Hi, Detective. What can I do for you?"

"I need you to check on lot number 7878, items seven and eight. Should be two rolls of nylon rope. Can you physically verify that these items are in your possession?"

"Sure, hold on." A few minutes pass before I get my answer. "Yep, they're here."

"Great. I'll email you the paperwork to move those items to the crime lab. I have suspicion that the items may be tied to a murder case. Can you get that done for me today?"

"No problem. Just as soon as I get your paperwork, they're on the way."

"Thanks, Larry."

My next call is to Andre LeBlanc's parole officer, David Branch. The call goes to his answering machine, and I leave a message. I know David from his work at the sheriff's office and courthouse. David started in law enforcement as a private investigator for a large law firm in Chicago and moved south to leave the cold and windy city behind. After working at the NOLA Police Department and later the sheriff's office, David eventually moved into a parole officer position, awaiting his retirement.

In a few minutes, David calls back, and he agrees to stop by my office before his first appointment at 9:30 a.m. After refreshing my coffee, I finish reading the information for a third time, when I notice David approaching my desk. After the regular formalities, David opens his file folder on Andre LeBlanc.

"So, Detective, you're asking about Andre LeBlanc. What information do you need from me?" David asks.

"I see in your report that he never showed up in February for his check-in. Have you heard from him since that date?"

"No, nothing. I'm sure you're aware that he has an outstanding warrant for failure to appear."

"Yes, I see that. How many times did you meet with him?"

"We met twice. He made his first two check-ins."

"He is a person of interest in a current murder case. What can you tell me about the person LeBlanc?"

"Off the record, I found him to be an extremely nervous person. Wouldn't make eye contact. Kept looking around. I personally felt he was either agitated or anxious about the whole situation. Maybe even scared at times."

"What do you mean scared?"

"He was hiding something. Like he was afraid of what I might find out. Always avoided talk about his future. He didn't trust me or the police. Said several times that we were out to get him. When I asked what he meant by that, he would just repeat the same statement. I don't think he trusts anyone."

"His being nervous doesn't fit a tattoo artist. He would need to be in control. Did he ever talk about friends or relatives or people at work?" I ask.

"No, he avoided talking about any relationships. But again, I felt he was hiding information. I perceived that he honestly believed that something or someone was coming down on him. That is why he felt intimidated by the police and my questioning."

"Did you have a psychological profile done on him?"

"No, we don't have the staff to cover a psychological profile. You understand how budgets work. Some of the most-needed areas are often the first to go."

"Yes, that's sad but true. Anything else you can tell me about him? Any quirks or characteristics you noticed?"

"Besides being nervous, he often touched the scar on his face. Like something he was constantly remembering. When I asked him about it, he said it was from a fight with someone over money. After a little bit more probing, he said it was over a drug deal that went bad. He wouldn't expound on that but laughed about the incident. Said the guy got what he deserved. When I asked him what he meant by that, he wouldn't say any more. I have to assume he may have done some real damage to the other guy."

"So you think he may be capable of becoming violent?"

"No question about that. When I pressured him a little, he had several outbursts and pushed some books off my desk. I'd say he has violent tendencies. I'm not a psychologist but just giving you my personal thoughts. All off the record."

"Thanks, David. If anything else comes to mind, please give me a call. We need to find this guy. I'll be going by his last known residence to see if I can find any more information. If I turn something up, I'll keep you informed."

After some small talk, David departs and leaves me with a pot boiling over with possibilities. Making note of LeBlanc's last residence, I hit the streets.

Upon arriving at the address, I find it's a concrete-block foundation on an overgrown empty lot. Judging by its location near Lake Pontchartrain and adjacent empty lots, whatever was here was destroyed back in 2005 by Katrina. That doesn't say much for NOLA's Police Department on verifying arrest addresses. Sadly, it's not the first time I've had this happen. The department is short of funds and short of people, and employees are overworked and underpaid. But the truth is, I wouldn't want to live anywhere else. I'm here for the long-term. So I just suck it up and do the best I can.

My next move is to his last place of employment. After parking in the Jackson Square area next to the St. Louis Cathedral, I take a short walk down Bourbon Street, turn left onto St. Phillip Street, and turn right onto North Rampart Street. Most of the stores in the district are open by ten o'clock in the morning, and tourist traffic is just starting to fill the sidewalks. A couple of barkers are pushing their wares and handing out discount tickets. A street person lies in front of an abandoned shop, wrapped in a torn blanket. His bony, unshaven face is propped up by a ball of rolled-up clothes. Street people and beggars are a common sight in the French Quarter District. Some can be dangerous, but most are just looking for a handout to help them survive another day. I've seen this guy before selling papers on the street to make a few bucks.

The smell of coffee and baked goods permeates the morning air. A wagon vendor pushes a red-painted cart of fruits and vegetables, making his morning deliveries. The picture reminds me of the 1958 Elvis Presley movie *King Creole*, a classic New Orleans musical drama. It depicts the cobblestone streets of New Orleans, with Elvis and a seafood vendor singing about the vendor's crawfish catch for sale.

Across the street, a shop owner sweeps the concrete sidewalk in front of his store and places a welcome mat outside his door. The white brick facade looks newly painted. T-shirts and hats hang in his display window. After passing Bar Tonique and the Voodoo Spiritual Temple, I enter Carnal Ink and approach a young man behind the counter.

"I'm looking for the owner. I'm Detective Dominic DeAngelis with the New Orleans Police Department. Is he here?"

"Yes, he's in the back. I'll get him for you."

Within minutes, a white-haired man appears.

"Name is Jim Carnes. I'm the owner here. What can I do for you?"

"I'm Detective Dominic DeAngelis with NOPD." I show him my badge and hand him one of my cards. "I have information that Andre LeBlanc worked here at one time. I want to ask you a few questions about him. Can we step into your office?"

"Sure, Detective. But you just missed him."

"What do you mean?"

"He was just by about twenty minutes ago. Came by to get some money I owed him."

"Did you give him a check or cash?"

"Always cash. These guys work as independent contractors. They all work on a percent of what they sell. It's a lot easier to keep track of that way."

"Was he driving or walking?"

"Don't know. Parking is around back."

"Do you have a security camera for the parking?"

"Well, yes, I do."

"I need to check the video."

He leads me to the back office, and I sit down and rewind the last thirty minutes of the DVD recorder. Nothing is revealed in the parking area. I then bring up the inside camera's footage. I see LeBlanc enter the shop and speak with Jim. Jim goes to the back, brings him some cash, and hands it to him. LeBlanc leaves on foot. There's no evidence of a vehicle through the front window on the DVD.

"He probably parked several blocks away and walked over," I say. "He did approach and leave from the left of the shop. Did he say anything that might have indicated where he was going?"

"No, just wanted his money. He seems to be an important guy. You're the second person looking for him this week."

"Who else is looking for him?"

Jim picks up a business card from the top of his desk. "Guy by the name of Justin Lancer with the *New Orleans Chronicle*. You know him?"

"Yes, I know him," I answer.

"He asked me to give him a call if LeBlanc showed up."

"I'll give him a call for you. I owe him one."

"What did LeBlanc do anyway? He seems to be getting a lot of attention lately."

"He's a person of interest in an ongoing investigation. You need to call me immediately if he shows up again. Anybody here hang out with him?"

"No, he was pretty much a loner."

"I'm going to need to take the inside DVD with me to search back any contacts he may have had in the shop. You have a problem with that, or do I need to get a warrant?"

"No, you can take it, but it won't do you any good."

"And why is that?"

"I record over each month. LeBlanc left a month ago. Today was the first time I've seen him since then."

"I'll take it anyway. He might have stopped by when you were out."

"Sure, if I see him again, I'll give you a call."

After leaving the shop, I head back into the French Quarter, following Royal Street for several blocks. Having grown up in New Orleans, I remember the French name *Vieux Carre*, meaning "Old Square," being used by the older Creoles. The neighborhood is the oldest in the city. The district today includes all the land stretching along the Mississippi River from Canal Street to Esplanade Avenue and inland to North Rampart Street. It equals an area of seventy-eight square blocks. Most of the old historic buildings date back to the eighteenth century, during the Spanish rule. In the distance, I can hear the calliope of the last authentic steam-powered boat on the Mississippi river. The steamboat *Natchez* serenades passersby in the French Quarter by playing its steam-powered organ three times a day.

Tourists and LSU football fans parade in the street, yelling at a shirtless man in shorts standing on a second-floor wrought iron–wrapped balcony and waving an Alabama Crimson Tide flag. Beer and whiskey are already flowing through the district as a couple of NOPD bicyclists cover their beat to keep some tone of peace on the street. Every few feet, I stop and survey the faces on both sides. I can't for the life of me comprehend all the different-colored hairstyles. Pink, blue, red, and yellow seem to dominate the culture. An occasional spiked rainbow head appears, accompanied by multiple face piercings and tattoos. *Weirdos* is the only word that comes to mind. It's not as if they have a loose screw in their heads; the screw has fallen out completely.

Just for a moment, my mind takes me back to my teen years. I was a hell-raiser, seeing how many bars and strip joints I could take on in a day's time, always ready for a verbal or physical fight. When liquor was involved, I feared no one. During one fight outside a shop, I knocked a man through one of the storefronts. By some miracle, he only needed a dozen stitches in the back of his leg. I was released from the police to my parents, as no charges were pressed, but I had to pay for the storefront. Shortly after that incident, I joined the Marines. I found out one thing quickly: I wasn't the baddest dude on the planet.

The streets haven't changed much. The same buildings are there, just a different color. The same knuckleheads are around, just thirty years later.

I grab a beer from the closest bar for show, pull out my shirttail, and unbutton my shirt. Since LeBlanc has some cash, he may be looking for some quick drugs or meeting up with someone. With some luck, I might find him since he doesn't know me.

Leaving the main circus, I walk the side streets, covering Barracks Street, Governor Nicholls Street, Ursulines Avenue, St. Phillip Street, and Dumaine. As I pass the New Orleans Historic Voodoo Museum on Dumaine, I see my man. He is standing across the street, on the corner of Bourbon Street and Dumaine. He appears to be waiting for someone.

I immediately slow my pace, walk to the nearest shop, and step inside. Through the storefront glass, I have a clear view. LeBlanc takes notice of my entry, and we make eye contact. Before I can get outside the door, he takes off down Bourbon Street.

Ditching my beer, I rush to the corner. I see only tourists on a crowded street. I know he'll easily disappear from the district in a matter of minutes. I curse myself for looking up when I did. *Stupid novice move.* I hang around the area for another thirty minutes, hoping someone might turn up looking to meet LeBlanc. If someone is there, the person never exposes him- or herself.

Heading back to my car, I pass through Jackson Square. Jackson Square is a historic park in the French Quarter. It was declared a national historic landmark in 1960 for its central role in the city's history. The center flagpole symbolizes the 1803 ceremonial transfers from Spain to France and then from France to the United States.

Following the 1815 Battle of New Orleans, the former military plaza was renamed Jackson Square for the battle's victorious General Jackson. In the center of the park stands an equestrian statue of Andrew Jackson erected in 1856. The statue was dedicated in a grand ceremony on Saturday, February 9, 1856. The square also has four slightly older statues representing the four seasons, one near each corner of the square.

On the north side of the square are three eighteenth-century historic buildings. The center of the three is the St. Louis Cathedral. The cathedral was designated as a minor basilica by Pope Paul VI. To its left is the Cabildo, the old city hall, now a museum, where the final version of the Louisiana Purchase was signed. To the cathedral's right is the Presbytère, built to match the Cabildo. The Presbytère was initially planned for housing the city's Roman Catholic priests and other church officials. At the start of the nineteenth century, it was adapted as a courthouse, and in the twentieth century, it also became a museum.

As I round the corner, I see two shady-looking white men in their early twenties leaning on my car. I grin and think to myself, *Come on, boys. Make my day.*

As I approach closer, one steps up onto the curb and slides a tool into his back pocket. I stop about ten feet away. "You boys need something out of my car?"

"Why, we just watching it for you, boss man. You know how bad the crime is in the city. I'd say you owe us ten for watching it." He laughs.

"I think ten is just about right," I reply. I reach into my pocket and pull out my badge. "You boys picked the wrong dude today. You see, I haven't killed anyone today, and I would like to make you an example. What do you say, boys? Is it a good day to die?"

"Why, Officer, are you threatening us?"

"Damn right I am. I don't have time to take you guys in right now, so here's how this deal will go down. You can go crawl back under the rock you came from, or I can call the coroner's office. Either way, I win. Now, boss man, what's it going to be?"

"Come on, man. Let's get out of here," replies the man leaning on the car.

I lift my shirttail and expose my handgun. "Your partner's smart.

Now, get the hell out of here, and don't let me catch you in this area again. I won't be so nice next time."

The man on the curb takes a sarcastic bow and motions to his buddy to move away. As soon as they have their backs turned toward me, I call dispatch and report the two car thieves, giving complete descriptions and their whereabouts. Within minutes, I see a NOPD car cruising the area.

Leaving the district, I drive by Harrah's New Orleans and find a parking spot. Taking a short walk, I check out the Fulton Street area. If I were looking to meet someone for a drug exchange, my second choice would be Fulton Street. My next choice would be the Riverwalk. Both areas are crowded and have easy access to multiple escape routes. I don't have much hope of seeing LeBlanc at either location, but I'm already here, so why not take a stroll and wish for luck?

Fulton Street is always packed with tourists and locals looking for cold beer and sports entertainment. The major draw is Archie Manning's Sports Bar and Grill. The Cajun-French phrase *"Laissez les bons temps rouler,"* or, as we say in English, "Let the good times roll," is what Manning's is all about. With cold beer, Cajun food, more than thirty flat-screen TVs, and two thirteen-foot megascreens, it is the perfect setting for game day. I've spoken with Archie several times over the years. He was born in Drew, Mississippi, and was named an all-American quarterback while at Ole Miss, where his number was retired. In 1971, he was the second player chosen in the NFL draft and the number-one pick of the New Orleans Saints. He concluded his fifteen-year career in 1985. The walls are loaded with pictures and memorabilia not only of him but also of his three sons, Peyton, Cooper, and Eli. Two of his sons, Peyton and Eli, played in the NFL after their college days, and both became Super Bowl winners, Peyton with Denver and Eli with the Giants.

Walking the beat, I don't notice anything out of the ordinary, except, of course, for the crazies with colored hair. As I peer into the glass storefront of every bar, nothing flags my attention. Leaving Fulton Street, I cross Convention Center Boulevard and cut through the parking lot to the Riverwalk Marketplace. The Marketplace is an indoor food court and mall along the Mississippi River. Taking note of everyone I pass, I decide to stop at Cane's Chicken Fingers to indulge in a little afternoon delight.

After ordering the fingers with crinkle-cut fries and a freshly squeezed lemonade, I sit at a food court table and watch the flow of people through the mall. I hear the brass bell sound at the Fudgery, alerting the shoppers that the fudge makers are about to pour out the hot fudge onto the cutting table and entertain the onlookers with singing and funny antics. As I dawdle with my food, I realize I'm procrastinating again. I take out my cell phone and call Justin. He answers on the third ring.

"Good afternoon, Detective. What can I do for you?"

"Well, let me start by saying I'm sorry for hanging up on you. I just felt you were overstepping your boundary. But I must admit that based on what little information I have gathered on LeBlanc, he's a person of interest. He may well be the witness who ties this case together."

"Thanks, Detective. I understand your reaction, but don't you think LeBlanc could be a lot more than just a witness?"

"I'm not making a judgment at this time about him, but my gut tells me we have the right person under arrest. Just how LeBlanc fits into the picture is still not clear. I'll tell you that he had in his possession two rolls of nylon rope, which I've sent to our lab for testing. I'm sure you're aware that a similar rope was used in the murders. I hope to have an answer on the rope by tomorrow. I'm figuring LeBlanc and Morone have some ties, but I'm still hanging my hat on Morone."

"Any luck on LeBlanc's whereabouts?" Justin asks.

"No, his last address was a dead end. I did see him from a distance in the French Quarter this morning, but he gave me the slip. He's on the run."

"If you're still in the district, he has a cousin who works at Vaping and Tattoos. Young guy named Willy. Bald head with a black widow tattoo on his cheek. He was the one who first put me onto LeBlanc."

"And why am I just hearing about this? This is the kind of stuff that pisses me off."

"Maybe because you hung up on me."

"Oh yeah, that. Touché," I reply.

"Anyway, Willy tried to call LeBlanc the day I was there but got a phone recording saying the number was no longer in service. I'm not sure now if it was a legitimate call or not. He may have called him after I left to warn him."

"Anything else you need to tell me?"

"No, not really. I have a second interview with Morone coming up tomorrow. I'll let you know how it goes."

"That'll work. I'll drop in on Mr. Willy while I'm here." The phone call disconnects. "Smart-ass." I laugh. Ditching the last half of my fries and drink, I check Google for the Vaping and Tattoos address, retrieve my car, and find a parking place about a block away from the shop.

As I approach the shop, I spot my bald-headed contact standing outside, puffing on an e-cigarette. "You Willy?"

"Tat me. You come fo' some stain, my man?"

"No, I'm Detective DeAngelis. I hear you have information on the whereabouts of your cousin Andre LeBlanc." I flash my credentials. "Is that right?"

"No, sir, tat ain't right. I don't know wer he is."

"Don't give me that crap! Either you come clean, or we'll take a little ride downtown for questioning. Now, what's it going to be?"

"No, sir. I swear. I don't know wer he is. Man, I lose my job. I don't know. I swear!"

"Yeah, when was the last time you saw him?"

"Ben tree or four month ago."

"And where was that?"

"He be in tha Quarter, talkin' with a chick."

"This chick have a name?"

"Ev'rybody got a name. Don't know hers."

"What did she look like?"

"Jus' a chick. Blue-spike hair. Some tats. 'Bout my size."

"And you haven't seen LeBlanc or her since then?"

"No, sir. I swear." Willy checks the shop through the storefront. "Can I go now? Boss be lookin' fo' me."

"One more question. Where was he staying?"

"Don't know. Nev' ben to his place."

"Try again!"

"Don't know. I swear. Don't know."

I pat my pockets as if looking for something and pull out my cell phone. "I don't have a card with me, so I'm going to send you my cell number. Call me if you hear or see either of them again. You got that?"

"Yes, sir."

"Give me your cell number, and I'll call you."

Willy hesitates for a moment and then gives me his number.

I dial the number, and nothing happens. "I must have heard you wrong. Try again, hot rod."

The second attempt rings his phone.

"One more thing," I say.

"Yes, sir?"

"Get off those e-cigarettes; they're bad for you." I smile.

"Yes, sir."

On the way back to my car, I call the office and leave Willy's cell number with the receptionist and ask her to have the officer on duty pull his call logs for the last four months. Maybe something will show up.

CHAPTER 5

While working late on my outline of questions for Morone the next morning, I get a call from Eric a little before eight o'clock.

"Justin, good news. There's a break in the Morone case. I have two rolls of nylon rope that were sent to the lab by Detective Dominic DeAngelis. The characteristics match those of the rope used in the murders. I don't know where he acquired them, but there's no doubt they match."

"That definitely adds to the case. I spoke to Dominic earlier today, and he told me he had sent the rope to the lab. I appreciate your giving me a heads-up. Is there any rope cut off the rolls?"

"No, they were both intact. They still had the plastic shrink-wrap on them when received."

"There's a third roll that is missing. This roll could be the murder weapon."

"Did these two rolls come from Morone?" Eric asks.

"No, they were found with another person by the name of LeBlanc. A warrant has been issued, but as of now, he hasn't been found."

"That's all I have, but if anything else turns up, I'll give you a call."

"Thanks, Eric. Take care."

The next morning, I arrive at the prison and fill out the paperwork that allows me to enter the guarded chamber. I'm patted down for a second time, and my credentials are checked again before I'm directed to room number six.

The room is approximately ten by twelve feet, made of cinder block walls painted light blue. A black metal door with a viewing window is the only entrance and exit. Four metal chairs are bolted to the gray concrete floor and surround a metal table with a locking handcuff device six inches in from the edge. The table is also bolted to the floor. The twelve-foot-high ceiling has two rolls of tube light fixtures recessed into the drywall. The lights have a plastic covering with wire mesh. Two red-painted ceiling pipes run the length of the room, containing two sprinkler heads. A smoke detector sits between the two light strings, centered above the table. A single air duct and intake duct penetrate the back wall, by the ceiling.

While I wait on the guard to bring in Morone, I look over my notes and check my tape recorder by recording the who, what, when, and where and playing it back. After a fifteen-minute wait, the door opens. A black guard leads Morone into the room, holding on to his right arm. Morone's ankle fetters slap the concrete floor as he shuffles over toward the chair. Once he's seated, the guard attaches Morone's handcuffs to the table's locking device and checks to see that it's secure.

"I'll be outside the door, watching through the viewing window. Let me know if you need anything," the guard says.

"Thank you, Officer," I reply.

Once the guard is outside, I turn my attention to Morone. His appearance has improved since our last meeting. The bruising on his arm and hand has almost disappeared. His hair is cut and clean. He sits more erect but leans back in the chair, disengaging himself. His eyes are alert, but his body language is clear.

"My name is Justin Lancer. Do you remember me from last week?"

"Yes, I remember you."

"I'm going to tape our conversation for my information only. It will not be used in a court of law or turned over to anyone. Do I have your approval to tape our conversation?"

"Yes."

"Please state your full name."

"Raymond Lester Morone."

"Mr. Morone, you have agreed to have our conversation taped today and understand that this tape will not be used against you in a court of law. Is that correct?"

"Yes."

"One of the first items I'd like to discuss is why there is no database information on you for the past thirty-seven years. Can you comment on the lack of information on your history?"

"Yeah, the system screwed up. Can't fix stupid." He smiles for the first time.

"No, I guess not." I return a smile. "Do you have any family members I can check with?"

"No, no family left."

"You told the police you grew up in Picayune, Mississippi, and graduated from Picayune High School. Is that correct?"

"Yes."

"I'm sure you know that Picayune High School burned down quite a few years ago with all its records."

"No, I didn't know that. I left home shortly after graduation and moved to New Orleans. Didn't keep up with Picayune news. Just glad to get out of there."

"What year did you graduate?"

"In 1999."

"Do you know if your parents are still living?"

"Nope. Don't care. Dad was a drunk, and we didn't see eye to eye. So I left. Never heard from them again."

"What about your mother?"

"She was weak. Supported him and not me. Not much to tell. She was probably glad when I left."

"According to the police report, your parents' names were Jim and Sheryl Morone. Is that correct?"

"Yes."

"What was your mother's maiden name?"

"Long. Sheryl Long."

"Where were you living at that time?"

"It was a small farmhouse on Route 43. About two miles out of town."

"What do you remember about the house?"

"Just a cracker-box farmhouse. Two bedrooms. One bath. White-painted slat boards. Fireplace. Covered porch. Small pond in back."

"Is the house still there?"

"Don't know."

I turn my attention back to his parents. "Do you know there is no information or grave site on either of your parents?"

"I already told you: you can't fix stupid."

"Do you remember any grandparents or other relatives?"

"None."

"What about friends? Who did you hang out with at school?"

"Bill Tamboli and I hung out."

"Did you keep in touch with him when you graduated?"

"No, he died in a car crash our senior year."

"What about girlfriends? Did you date anyone in high school?"

"Nope. Too busy taking care of the house and fighting with the drunk."

"Raymond, you're not giving me much to work with here. If you want my help, you have to work with me."

Raymond shifts in his chair and appears to be getting annoyed with this line of questioning, so I flip through my notes, change the subject, and give him a couple of minutes to relax.

"Do you remember where you were on January 1 of this year?"

"Nope."

"Do you know a person by the name of William Sutton? Has a

tattoo of a two-headed snake on his neck and goes by the name of Viper?"

"Nope."

"Viper has identified you as being at the Grand Mart Motel in Metairie on January 1. That is the work location of the first victim you're charged with killing. Have you ever been to the Grand Mart Motel?"

"Don't think so."

"Did you have contact with a clerk at the motel by the name of Elizabeth Mary DeBoy?"

"Nope."

There is no change in his posture. I don't observe any flex in muscle tone or eye movement. Looking over my notes, I check my list for the other dates and victims' names.

"Do you remember where you were on February 11?"

"Nope."

"How about March 13? Do you remember where you were?"

"Nope."

"Did you have contact with a nurse by the name of Mary Sadler Cotton who worked at Picayune General Hospital in New Orleans?"

"Don't think so."

"Did you have contact with a clerk at a twenty-four-hour market near the airport by the name of Teresa Elaine McCall?"

"Don't think so."

With no change in body language, I change my approach. I stand up, pick up my notebook, and walk to the back wall. Flipping through several pages, I start again. "What kind of work do you do, Raymond?"

"Small construction jobs. Mostly home repair."

"You mean like drywall, painting, plumbing—stuff like that?"

"Yeah, that's right."

"Man, I always hated doing drywall. Never could get the joints to look right. What's the secret?"

Raymond leans forward. "Patience. Just patience. Can't rush drywall mud. Needs to sit a day between coats."

"Do you ever have someone help you on a job?"

"Every now and then. Not too often."

"Do you ever do any welding?"

"Yeah, mostly handrails and wrought iron gates. Small stuff."

I flip another couple of pages in my notebook and walk along the back wall. "Do you know a tattoo artist by the name of Andre LeBlanc?"

Raymond leans back in his chair again, distancing himself from me. "Yes."

"How do you know Mr. Andre LeBlanc?"

"He did a tattoo for me."

"How many times did you see Mr. LeBlanc?" I notice Raymond's hands close to form fists, and his knuckles turn white.

"I don't know."

"More than two? Did you see him more than two times?"

"Yeah, more than two."

"How many times would you say? More than five?"

"Yeah, maybe." Raymond shifts in his chair for the first time.

"Did he ever ride in your truck?"

"Yeah, a couple of times with a chick he was tattooing."

"Did this chick have a name?"

"Don't remember."

"What did she look like?"

"Don't remember much. Blonde, I think. Pretty average looking. Nothing special."

"Did you ever loan Mr. LeBlanc your truck?"

Raymond shifts again in his chair. "Yeah, a couple of times."

"Has Mr. LeBlanc ever been in your apartment?"

"Yeah, a couple of times."

"Did he ever have his lady friend with him when he was in your apartment?"

"Don't know. I wasn't there."

"You guys must have been pretty close if you gave him a key to your apartment when you weren't there."

"He helps me out sometimes, and I returned the favor."

"Are you protecting him?"

"From what?"

"You do realize you're up on three charges of murder, don't you?"

"Yes, I know that."

"The evidence against you is starting to grow. There's DNA evidence putting one of the victims in your truck and apartment. And you're telling me you have no knowledge of this?"

"I told you I don't know!"

I walk back to my chair and lean on its back. His fists tighten again, and I can tell he's getting agitated. I flip through the pages in my notebook as if looking for something and give him time to relax by changing the subject. "Do you smoke?"

"That's a dumb-ass question. What does that have to do with anything?"

"Maybe nothing. Maybe everything. Do you smoke?"

"No, I don't smoke or do drugs. Don't know what you're getting these days. Too much bad stuff on the street. Can't trust anyone."

"You must have trusted LeBlanc to loan him your truck and keys."

"Yeah, that was a mistake."

I take my seat and spend a few minutes in silence. Once I observe Morone make eye contact, I continue my questioning. "Tell me about LeBlanc."

"Met him last year in the Quarter. He was sitting at a bar, scribbling a drawing on a napkin. We talked awhile, and he bought me a beer. He told me he was a tattoo artist and showed me what he was drawing. It was a cool drawing of Taurus the bull. It was damn good too. He seemed like an okay guy, and I ran into him a couple more times. He invited me to his shop and showed me his binder of designs. He said if I ever needed some help to let him know. So he helped me several times. Not much more to tell."

"What kind of work did he help you with?"

"Just normal stuff."

"What about welding? Did he ever help you with any welding?"

"I don't know. Maybe."

"Raymond, this might be very important. Try to remember. Did he help you with any welding?"

"I can't remember."

"What was the last welding job you did?"

"I think it was a wrought iron gate that had come off its hinges. Yeah, I'm sure that was the last one."

"Do you remember when that was?"

"It was around Christmas. Yeah, just before Christmas."

"So that would have been December of last year?"

"Yeah, that's right."

"And did Andre LeBlanc help you?"

"Yeah, he helped hold the gate while I did some welding."

"So he would have used some welding gloves at that time?"

"Maybe, or just some leather gloves to hold the gate."

"How many pairs of welding gloves do you have?"

"Don't know. Maybe two or three."

"Do you carry them in your truck?"

"Yeah, that's right."

I stand up again and walk over to the back wall. "Have you noticed if a pair of gloves is missing from your truck?"

"No, I haven't done a job where I needed them."

"Let's talk again about the woman who was with him. You said she was just average. Do you remember what she was wearing?"

"Blue jeans and a T-shirt, I think."

"Anything embroidered on the jeans or printed on the T-shirt that you remember?"

"There was something on the T-shirt, but I don't remember what it was."

"Do you remember what color it was?"

"No, not really. Dark—maybe black or blue."

"Was she wearing a necklace or earrings?"

"Don't know. Didn't pay that much attention to her."

"Any tattoos on her arms or face?"

"I think she had some on her arms."

"Do you remember what they were?"

"No, I didn't look them over, if that's what you mean."

"Wasn't she next to you in the truck?"

"No, Andre was sitting next to me. She was sitting on the passenger side."

"Do you remember her name?"

"No, I don't remember."

The next thirty minutes are much the same. I go over the same questions but ask them in a different way. The only discrepancy I note is that Raymond states that the girl in the truck was sitting next to him instead of on the passenger side. When I bring this up, he says he can't remember for sure. I let him sit in silence for a while as I walk around the room. He remains calm and shifts in his chair several times but doesn't look up or speak.

"Raymond, I think we are about through. I just have one more item to ask about. Do you ever use nylon rope in your business or at home?"

Raymond changes his posture but remains silent. I check my watch's second hand as it ticks away. As hard as it is for me not to speak, I know that to break the silence would mean a loss of the question. Seventeen seconds tick by before he answers.

"No."

We set another meeting for next week, and I ask a couple more questions about his parents but receive no new information. His childhood wasn't pleasant, and he shows no remorse over leaving his parents behind. There remains the question of identity. The only way to resolve this issue, if it can be resolved, is to take a trip to Picayune. Maybe I can locate the farmhouse and dig up some information from the courthouse and archives that will lay bare the issue. If nothing else, I might need to search the cemeteries in the area to locate grave sites of his relatives or parents.

By the time I leave the prison, it's almost noon. As I'm preparing to call Dominic, I receive a call from Kate in Hawaii.

"Hey, Kate. How are you doing in Hawaii?"

"Things are good here. I hope to head home in a couple of weeks.

Most of my shots of Kilauea are finished. Next week, my plan is to start shooting the lava tubes as they flow into the ocean. Kilauea is awesome and scary. From the helicopter, you can feel the intense heat from the lava flows. The changes in atmospheric temperature cause a lot of air turbulence. It can be dangerous if you get too close. Several times, we had to pull out and approach from another angle. I'm ready to come home."

"That's great news. I've missed spending time together. Do you know how long you'll be home?"

"I'm not sure, but I would like to talk with you about something important."

"Well, you definitely have my attention. What's up?"

"I received a call from Tulane University. They want me to interview for a position to head up the photography department."

My heart skips a beat. "Kate, that would be fantastic! How do you feel about not freelancing anymore?"

"I'm not sure right now. It sounds intriguing, but I need to find out more about what it will entail. I've enjoyed the travel, but I could use a change. It could be my dream job."

"I know I'm being somewhat selfish when I say this, but I'd love to have you here. You know how I feel about you, but you need to do what's right for you."

"I know, Justin. I miss our times together too. We can talk more when I get back and see where the interview leads. I'm excited and a little scared. I'd hate to make a wrong decision."

"You know what my dad says: 'You make a decision, and then you make it right.'"

"Yes, I remember you telling me that before. There's a lot of wisdom in that statement."

"Yes, and the older I get, the more I understand what it means."

"Well, I have to go get ready for my next shoot. I'll see you soon."

"Please be careful, and bring some award-winning pictures home."

"I will. How is your investigation going?"

"I had my first interview today with my client. There're a lot of unanswered questions. I'm heading to Picayune, Mississippi, to see if I can find some answers. In the meantime, the police are still searching for an important witness who is crucial to the case. So far, he can't be found."

"I'm sure you'll find what you are looking for. Miss you, and see you soon."

"Miss you too. Let me know your return schedule, and I'll pick you up at the airport."

"Thank you. I will."

After I hang up, I sit and stare at the phone for several minutes. Thoughts of my time with Kate race through my mind. It's as if I'm watching a motion picture as memories flash across the big screen.

I remember sitting out on the beach with Kate. The Gulf waves gently cover the white sand only to depart back into the ocean, leaving behind a wet sparkle on the grains that maintain their place. Glancing over the water to the horizon, I can see the ends of the earth, where the rainbow rests.

I believe that was the day when my mind and heart coexisted and became consubstantial with each other.

The spell is broken as my body jerks, and my phone announces an incoming call. Dominic is identified as the perpetrator. I take a deep breath and push the connect button.

CHAPTER 6

"Good afternoon, Detective. I'm just leaving the jail."

"So give me the skinny. Any new information from Morone?" asks Dominic.

"No, not much. As I'm sure you know, he grew up in Picayune and left his parents after high school graduation. Moved to NOLA and started a handyman business. He met Andre LeBlanc last year and loaned him his car and apartment in exchange for some work help and tattooing. He told me that LeBlanc had a girl with him once when they were in his truck, but he couldn't describe her or remember her name. If this girl was one of the victims, it would explain her prints in Morone's truck and her DNA at his apartment. He could also be covering for LeBlanc, but that makes no sense, knowing that he's up on a murder charge. He still claims the missing information on him is not his fault. He completely denies knowing any of the victims or being at the motel where Viper claims to have seen him. I'm going to take a trip to Picayune and dig around the archives. Maybe I can find some missing information on him or his parents."

"Yeah, I agree with you about Morone. He's not stupid. There's no reason to take the rap for LeBlanc when his own life is at stake. But there's more between these two than Morone is telling. If Morone is not coming clean, we have to find LeBlanc."

"Nothing on his whereabouts?"

"Nothing yet, but we'll find him."

"You want to meet up tomorrow? I'd like to talk more about the other victims."

"Sure, we can do that. Give me a call."

Working my way over to Highway 59 in New Orleans, I head northeast toward Picayune. The city is located approximately forty-five miles from New Orleans and is the largest city in Pearl River County, Mississippi, with a population of just more than ten thousand. Taking the Picayune exit, I find my way to Goodyear Boulevard and locate Margaret Reed Cosby Memorial Library, which serves as the headquarters of the Pearl River County library system. I've always found that the local library is the best place for research in an area. Not only does it have years' worth of public information, but the librarian can usually direct you to the local patriarchs who love to share their knowledge.

Entering the library, I locate the librarian on duty and introduce myself. He introduces himself as Ned Beasley. I explain that I'm researching a family by the name of Morone and information on Picayune High School. He directs me to the newspaper archives and explains the layout of the library system. He informs me that the original high school burned down in 2003, but the library has some of the high school's yearbooks dating back to 1990, before the new high school was built. The courthouse also has some pictures on the wall of older graduating classes dating back to the 1950s.

Searching the newspaper archives, I find the story of the high school fire in the *Times-Picayune*. The school burned down on July 12, 2003. According to the article, arson was suspected, but no arrests were made. I make a copy of the article and then move to the reference section to find the yearbooks. Morone told me he graduated in 1999. On the reference shelf, all the yearbooks are in order, except for 1999. It's missing from the bookcase. I check three prior yearbooks and glance through the pictures to determine if any student's picture resembles Morone. Nothing matches up.

I approach the librarian with the missing book information, and Ned checks the library database and reports that the book was reported missing on the December 2017 inventory. A replacement was never donated.

I ask if he knows anyone who grew up in the area who might have knowledge of the Morone or Tamboli family. Ned gives me a name: Bo Watkins. Mr. Watkins runs a general store and farm that go back three generations. Bo is now in his eighties and lives on his family's farm outside Picayune, on Route 43, the same route Morone said he lived on.

Ned tells me it's a white house with a red roof about three miles out. "Only red roof on Route 43. House is on the left."

I thank him for the information and return to searching the archives. This time, I do a second search in the *Times-Picayune* for 1999. I get a hit on a William Tamboli. William was killed in a car crash on Route 43 in June of the same year. According to the article, a truck traveling south crashed head-on into William Tamboli's car. Both drivers were killed. The investigation revealed that the driver of the truck had been drinking and crossed over into the oncoming lane. The truck driver was Dwayne Johnson of New Orleans, age fifty-nine. William Tamboli's address was listed as Route 43, Picayune, Mississippi. His parents were John and Alice Tamboli. William Tamboli was buried in Memorial Gardens Cemetery in Picayune.

I also check the years 2003 and 2004 to see if anyone was ever arrested or convicted of arson in the high school fire. In July 2004, a year after the fire, an arson investigator was interviewed by the *Times-Picayune* and confirmed that an accelerant was used in the fire, but there were no suspects or arrests.

My next stop is the courthouse. Checking in with the property tax and assessment clerk, I'm able to search, by name, property owners for both the city and county. Again, I find a dead end—nothing under the name of Morone or Tamboli.

Feeling slightly encouraged by the new article information, I head out of Picayune on Route 43 to find Mr. Bo Watkins. Route 43 is a two-lane paved road that runs north, parallel to the Pearl River. The Pearl River is the dividing line between southwestern Mississippi and Louisiana.

The landscape along Route 43 is made up of farmland on both sides. Except for an occasional fence, it's hard to tell where one farm ends and another begins. Farmhouses appear around every quarter mile along the stretch of road. Watching the mailboxes along the way, I find one marked "Watkins" three miles outside Picayune. The house is a white-painted wood frame with a red metal roof. Pulling into the gravel-covered driveway, I notice a man sitting on the porch. I pull closer to the house, stop, and step out of my car. A barrel of a man yells out.

"Don't need to be saved! Don't need no insurance! Don't need to buy anything! And no, this place is not for sale." He's dressed in bib overalls and a white T-shirt. His ruddy face is unshaven. He has a can of beer in his hand, and a bluetick coonhound lies at his feet.

"Then you're in luck," I respond. "I'm not a preacher or selling anything. I'm trying to find some information on a family by the name of Morone. I have information that they lived out here some years back. My name is Justin Lancer with the *NOLA Chronicle*. Mr. Ned Beasley at the library gave me your name and said you might be able to help me."

As I approach the bottom of the porch steps, the coonhound starts to growl. "Will your dog bite?" I ask.

"Probably if you bite him first. Ole Jake don't get around much anymore. Got his leg caught in a hog trap some years back. Can't move very fast. You'll be fine if you stay off the porch. Ole Jake has gotten fat and lazy. Just lays around and farts all day. Estell makes us come out here when she's cooking. Says she doesn't know which one of us is stinking up the place." Bo leans forward in his chair and lowers his voice. "Gets nice and quiet for the both of us out here." He grins. "Sometimes I think ole Jake does it on purpose."

"Who you talking with out there?" shouts a loud voice from inside the screen door.

"Fellow here looking for a family by the name of Mahoney," Bo replies.

"Don't know them!" Estell yells back.

"The family name is Morone. Jim and Sheryl Morone!" I yell back at the door. "Used to live out here on Route 43."

"Don't know them either," the voice replies.

Turning my questions back to Bo, I try again. "Mr. Watkins, have you lived here all your life?"

"Well, hell no, not yet." He laughs and takes a drink of his beer. "Haven't used that one in a long time. What'd you think, Jake? Did I get him?" Jake lifts his head for a moment and looks at Bo before reclining to his last position. "To answer your question, this farm was my grandfather's. One hundred twenty acres of prime black soil. Goes all the way back to the Pearl River. Raised a little bit of everything in its day. Now I rent it out to sharecroppers. Me and ole Jake just sit back and let somebody else do the work. What's your name again?"

"Justin. Justin Lancer."

"And who are you looking for?"

"Jim and Sheryl Morone. They were supposed to have a farm about two miles outside Picayune. Had a small pond in the back."

"There was an old farmhouse that burned down about ten years ago. The house was back a way on the other side of the road. But the land was owned by a man with the name of Roberts. Charles Roberts, I believe. He did rent the land out to some sharecroppers. Can't remember their name, but Morone doesn't sound right. It was an Italian name. Something like Stomboli. Had a kid who was killed in a car crash just up the road from here."

"Could it be Tamboli?" I ask.

"Yeah, that's it. Jim and Alice Tamboli. Just about a mile back toward town. You can still see part of the old brick chimney."

"Could it have been John instead of Jim?"

Bo yells at Estell inside. "Estell, what was the Tambolis' names who lived down the road? You know, the ones who had the son killed in a car crash."

"Their name was John and Alice. The boy was Bill."

"Yeah, that's what I said." Bo grins. "John and Alice."

"Do you know what ever happened to them?"

"No, not really. After their son was killed, they moved somewhere else. They were like gypsies. Traveled up and down the eastern US as different crops came in harvest. Really sad about their son. Had just graduated high school. Yes, sir, sad day."

"Did they ever find out what started the fire?"

"No, nobody was living there at the time. Probably some kid playing around inside. Never heard much more about it."

"Supper's about ready!" shouts the ghost voice from inside. "You want me to set another plate for your friend?"

"No, thanks, Mrs. Watkins!" I yell back to the door. "I'd like to get back to New Orleans before it gets dark, but thank you for the offer."

Turning my attention back to Bo, I thank him for his time. "You've been a great help to me. I was searching for one family but found another."

Bo raises his beer and takes the last drink. "Glad me and ole Jake could be of service."

Heading back toward Picayune, I spot a grassy field with a drive on the left side of the road. Pulling onto the field, I can see the remnants of a brick chimney. A small pond is visible between the trees lining the back of the field. I set the coordinates on my GPS so I can get an overhead view of the property on Google Earth when I get back home.

Once I get back into town, I locate Picayune Memorial Gardens Cemetery in the hope of finding the grave site of William Tamboli. Pulling into the cemetery parking lot, I notice there's no office building. Without a location plot, it will be almost impossible to locate the Tamboli grave. I try calling the office but get a recording that they close at 3:30 p.m. I add another item to my things-to-do list and head back to New Orleans.

)

On the way back, I talk with Dominic, and we agree to meet at the New Orleans Food and Spirit Restaurant on Lee Lane in Covington.

From Picayune, I take I-59 South toward New Orleans and pick up I-12 West. Once on the Northshore, I take Highway 190 into Covington and work my way over to Lee Lane. As I pull into the parking lot, I see Dominic entering the restaurant. Once inside, I head to the back wall in the bar area and take a seat at Dominic's table.

We exchange greetings just as the waiter approaches our table with menus and takes our drink order. Dominic orders red wine, and I opt for unsweetened tea. The place is filling fast and buzzing with locals. All the stools are taken at the oyster bar, and two young men talk and laugh with the customers as they place the oyster shells on a large, round metal pie plate filled with ice.

After talking briefly about his day, Dominic inquires about my trip to Picayune. "So how was your trip? I've been looking forward to speaking with you. Did you find any new information concerning the Morone investigation?"

"Well, yes and no. There's still a lack of information on the Morone name. In 2003, there was a fire at the high school that destroyed all the records. It was later confirmed as an act of arson. The childhood house that Raymond claimed he grew up in was occupied at the time by a family of sharecroppers by the name of Tamboli. That house was also destroyed in a fire, around 2008. One interesting item on Morone's identity is that the high school yearbook for 1999 is missing from the local library, the year he said he graduated. I'm going to put an ad on *Craig's List* to see if I can find another one."

"Someone is going to a lot of trouble to erase the past," Dominic says.

"Yes, it seems that way. When I interviewed Morone, he told me his best friend in high school was Bill Tamboli. Bill was killed in a car accident their senior year. I found an article in the *Times-Picayune* from 1999 that confirms the story. Bill is buried in the local cemetery, but I didn't have time to locate his grave. I'll need to make another trip to do that. His parents moved shortly after his death. I'll try to find them on the internet, but if they were sharecroppers, it could be an impossible task."

The waiter returns with our drinks, and we place our food orders.

Dominic orders eggplant stuffed with shrimp and crabmeat, and I order crab cakes topped with crawfish Pontchartrain sauce.

"You can do what you want, but I don't see that this Tamboli kid has any bearing on the Morone case," Dominic says. "The boy died eighteen years ago. You're wasting your time. Our high card is in finding LeBlanc. Morone and LeBlanc are tied together in this case. When we find LeBlanc, they both could get the chair. We'll find him. LeBlanc's cousin Willy had some calls on his cell phone that were traced back to phone cards you can buy anywhere. Judging by the dates, my guess is that they were calls to LeBlanc. We have a tail on Willy. He's scared. He'll mess up sooner or later and lead us to LeBlanc. In the meantime, I'll ask you to stay away from him. We need him to feel safe."

"I understand. But just so you know, I'm pursuing the information on the Tamboli family. I think there's something here we're missing."

"Suit yourself, but you're wasting your time."

I'm getting a little irritated with Dominic's criticism. "You thought it was a waste of time when I brought you the information on Leblanc. Now you seem to think he's involved somehow."

Dominic looks at me for a moment and takes a sip of wine, as if taking time to choose his words. "If you're looking for credit, I'll have to pass. We would have been drawn to LeBlanc sooner or later. So you can stop patting yourself on the back."

"Really? I thought you told me the case was closed. Sounds like you may have changed your mind." I see his jaw tighten, but he remains silent.

He raises his wineglass and smiles. "You're an arrogant little SOB, but you made your point. Keep me posted."

"I'll do that," I reply.

Dominic swirls the last bit of wine and empties his glass.

Seizing the opportunity to change the subject, I focus on my questions regarding the second victim. "I'd like to ask you some background information about the second victim in the Morone case. Would that be okay?"

"Sure, go ahead. I'll tell you what I can."

"If I remember correctly, the second victim was Mary Sadler Cotton. She was murdered on February 11 and worked at Picayune General Hospital in New Orleans. What else can you tell me about her?"

"Age thirty-seven. Single. Lived by herself in the Blue Creek Apartments in Mandeville. Grew up and went to school in St. Louis. Got her nursing degree in Memphis and moved to Mandeville in 2017. Apartment was clean. Not much there. Both parents deceased. Neighbors said they saw her on occasion. Always alone. We sent her cell phone and computer to Atlanta. It'll be a while before we get any info back."

"What about work friends? She must have spent time with someone at the hospital."

"She worked a four-day rotating shift. A lot of time in the ER at night. Her supervisor said she was dedicated to her work but didn't spend a lot of time with other nurses or doctors. Said she didn't know of any social activity with anyone on the floor. Just did her job and went home. If she had a social life, she kept it to herself."

"With a four-day work week, she had a lot of free time to socialize."

The waiter brings our food and checks on our drinks. Dominic orders another glass of wine and waits for the waiter to leave before continuing the conversation.

"You'd think that. I did find out that several of the bartenders in the French Quarter recognized her picture but didn't remember if she was with anyone or not. They usually aren't much help with information, considering the number of people they get in at night."

"You mentioned that her apartment was clean. No prints or DNA there or in her car?"

"No, nothing."

"Strange that prints and DNA were found with the first victim but not the second. What do you make of it?"

"Not unusual. Sometimes a serial killer will get better with time. He may realize he left something behind and compensate moving forward."

"It could also indicate that it's not the same person."

"Not a chance. The rope and MO are the same. Morone is our

guy, but LeBlanc is most likely involved. Once we find him, all your questions will be answered."

The waiter drops by with Dominic's wine and checks on our food. The table is quiet for a while as we chow down.

Dominic lifts his glass in a toast and smiles. "Good hunting."

After finishing dinner with Dominic, I decide to drive by Café Reconcile in the hope of catching up with John the Baptist. I know the café will be closed, but maybe he'll be helping with cleanup. It's not far out of my way, and John might have some new information on LeBlanc.

After crossing the Causeway Bridge, I pick up I-10 toward New Orleans and follow US-90 Business to Oretha Castle Haley Boulevard. As I near the café, I can see John standing outside the front door. I pull up to the curb, and John immediately recognizes me. He's dressed in black shorts with a red Café Reconcile T-shirt. His wood crucifix dangles around his neck. His smile is contagious.

"Good evening, Mr. Lancer," he says as he opens the passenger-side door. His left hand struggles to balance his tattered Bible and a cup of coffee. "So nice to see you again. May I step in?"

"Sure, John, take a seat."

Upon entering my car, he continues. "You can't park here on the main street, but if you want to drive around back, we can talk there."

"Sure," I reply. "I just wanted to stop by to see if you had any information on Andre LeBlanc."

"Not much. I contacted my friend at the police department, but he told me the reports were active and locked down. Another friend knows him from the tattoo shop. Said he saw him about a week ago in the French Quarter. LeBlanc was arguing with a young bald-headed man with a spiderweb tattoo on his head. There was some money exchanged, and they split. He reported that neither one looked happy."

"The kid with the bald head is LeBlanc's cousin Willy. The police have him under surveillance. They hope he'll lead them to LeBlanc. Anyone seen him since?"

"No, that was it. I know it's not much, but Mr. LeBlanc is not homeless, or he would have been by the mission. Either he's found a place to stay, or he's not in the area anymore."

"I think you're right. My bet is he's not in NOLA."

John sips his coffee before continuing. "You certainly live an exciting life, Mr. Lancer. I'll continue to ask around. Maybe when this is all over, you can award me with a Dick Tracy badge. I always wanted one of those." He laughs.

"Aren't you a little young to know Dick Tracy?"

"As one of my many passions, I'm an avid comic book reader. Superheroes and comic book villains are my specialty. It also helps with the homeless people. They love to hear a good hero story. Gives them hope."

"John, you're an amazing person." I laugh. "By the way, I downloaded the book you recommended by Og Mandino. You certainly qualify as a ragpicker. The work you do among the homeless is extraordinary. What possessed you to step into that kind of ministry?"

"Most people don't see the homeless. They're invisible to them. We'll always have the poor and homeless. Every person's situation is different, which means ending homelessness needs to be different for each person. The homeless are vulnerable. They feel lost and unloved. Hurricane Katrina left many in New Orleans homeless with nowhere to turn. In 2011, New Orleans had more than sixty-five hundred people who were homeless, making the city's rate of homelessness the highest in the United States. That same year, the city released a ten-year plan to end homelessness. Today that number has been lowered by eighty-five percent. Nationally, people who are homeless are counted every year in January through a process called the Point-in-Time, or PIT. As of January 2018, there were three thousand fifty-nine people homeless in Louisiana. In Jefferson and Orleans parishes, one thousand one hundred seventy-nine people are homeless. In New Orleans, the majority of our homeless are centered in the Central Business District and French Quarter. The amount of people who are homeless in a small area gives the appearance that we have a high rate of homelessness. In reality, New Orleans has a rate of three hundred two people homeless for every one hundred thousand residents, which is much lower than many cities across the country."

"So your mission as a ragpicker is to give hope and encouragement."

"Bingo, Mr. Lancer. Some of the homeless have mental issues, but most are spiritually sick, and their spirits are broken. In Mark chapter 2, Jesus speaks of healing. He said that those who are well do not need a physician, but the sick do. He came not to the call of the righteous but sinners. That includes me and you, Mr. Lancer."

"John, you always seem to give a lesson, and I don't even know I'm getting it." I laugh.

"Be careful, Mr. Lancer; your halo is starting to show." He smiles.

"Thanks for the information. Is there anything I can do for you? Can I drop you off somewhere?"

"No, thank you. I'm corner-preaching tonight." He laughs. "Tomorrow I'm heading over to the St. Louis Cemetery to visit my family's grave site."

"That wouldn't be Cemetery No. 1, would it?"

"Yes, that's right. Do you have family there?"

"No, I don't, but I'd like to tag along if possible. I know the archdiocese doesn't allow visitors except for tours and family members. Just so you know, I'd like to get a picture of Marie Laveau's grave. It will help with the articles I've been working on. It will also make my boss incredibly happy." I laugh.

"As long as it's for curiosity, I don't see any harm in it. Tomorrow it is, Mr. Lancer. I'll meet you there at nine o'clock tomorrow morning."

"Great. I appreciate your doing this."

"You're welcome. Now, how about tonight? Are you up for some corner preaching? You're welcome to come along."

"Give me a rain check on that. I would like to hear you sometime, but right now, I've got a lot of follow-up work to do at home. Take care, and stay safe."

"A rain check it is. I'll keep you posted if any more information becomes available." After exiting my car, John hits the street and disappears into the back alley.

When I get home, I pour a tall glass of iced tea and settle in at my workstation. Three items are on my list for this evening: I want to do a search on Mary Sadler Cotton to find out more information on her family, check online with Find a Grave to locate William Tamboli's grave, and go on Google Earth to look over the piece of land that was Tamboli's family's home in Picayune.

Starting with Google Earth, I use the coordinates I retrieved from my trip and enter them into the Google program. Within seconds, I get an overhead view of the property. Circling my cursor, I find that outline traces of the house can still be seen, along with fragments of the brick fireplace. Along the back of the property are a row of trees and a small pond. I also notice a small square object in front of the tree line. When I zoom in, the object appears to be a cover of some sort, maybe for a pump or well. There is also a pile of brush near the pond, which might contain trash from the burned house—something else to check out on my next trip to Picayune.

Next, I pull up Find a Grave and insert the information I have on William Tamboli. A picture of his headstone is displayed from the Picayune Memorial Gardens. From this, I'm able to pull up the coordinates and enter them into Google Earth. Zooming out, I get a location reference for my next trip. Zooming in, I can see slight details on the headstone, but the name and dates are not readable. I also notice a small area that appears to be damaged. Not able to get a clear resolution on the item, I add it to my list.

My final item is to search Mary Sadler Cotton. Using an ancestry search engine, I'm able to pull up Mary's family history. She was born in St. Louis on June 20, 1980, to Albert Ray Cotton and Estelle Louisa Thomas. Dominic's information that she moved to Mandeville in 2017 is correct, but there's something he missed: when she first moved to the area in 2017, according to a copy of her car registration, she lived in Picayune before finding the apartments in Mandeville. I jot down the address on my Picayune list. This might mean nothing, but it's amazing how this place is becoming a common epicenter.

After shutting down my computer, I organize my notes and decide to make another Picayune trip tomorrow after I meet with John.

CHAPTER 7

After arriving at the St. Louis Cemetery No. 1 on Basin Street a little early, I park in a pay lot across the street from the visitors' center. I cross over to the center and pick up some information on the cemetery for background information. Three Roman Catholic cemeteries in New Orleans are named St. Louis Cemetery. Due to the city's high water table, all burials are above ground. St. Louis Cemetery No. 1 is the oldest of the three. It was opened in 1789, replacing the city's older St. Peter Cemetery when the city was redesigned after the fire in 1788. The Diocese of New Orleans closed the cemetery to the general public in 2015 due to vandalism. Access is only permitted for tour groups and those who have family members interred there. St. Louis Cemetery No. 1 and No. 2 are included on the National Register of Historic Places.

Taking a few brochures, I head over to the cemetery entrance. As I approach, I see John speaking with the guard at the gate. John is dressed in a pair of black shorts held up with a rope belt and a lime-green T-shirt. He is wearing sandals and is carrying his tattered Bible. His normally ungroomed beard and hair are in reasonable order.

Around his neck is his wooden crucifix, hanging from a piece of string. The guard returns John's pass card and makes some notes on his clipboard.

"How long do you think you'll be, John?" asks the guard.

"Not long, sir. Less than an hour," John replies.

The guard turns to me and asks for an ID. I hand him my driver's license, and he makes additional notes and returns my license. "John, I've known you for several years, and I'm not going to ask you if this gentleman with you is a relative. I'm just going to assume he is and look the other way. Go right in."

"Thank you, sir." John smiles. "I'll take good care of him."

As we enter the gate, I'm in awe of the stone vaults to my left. I stop for a moment to take in the beautiful artwork.

"First time here, Mr. Lancer?" John asks.

"Yes, it is. This place is amazing. I've only seen pictures of the stonework in this cemetery, but they don't do it justice. These vaults are amazing."

"Yes, they are. Some of these are called oven vaults. They have stacked graves inside the vaults like oven racks, one above another. They house the remains of countless family members. Once the body is interred in a grave for one year and one day, the remains can be pushed to the back of the tomb, leaving room for another family member. I've been told that the grave plots here cost forty thousand dollars."

"I had no idea."

As we walk through the cemetery, it's hard to describe the majesty of some of the vaults. Some date back to the 1700s. Off to my left, I see a white stone pyramid. "What in the world is that?"

John smiles. "That, Mr. Lancer, is the future tomb of Nicolas Cage, the actor."

"Can we look at it?"

"Absolutely. Nicolas Cage is only in his fifties, but he loves New Orleans and wanted to be buried here. The mausoleum pyramid is nine feet tall. It's a beautiful structure but doesn't seem to fit among the older architecture."

"That inscription on the tomb. What does it mean?"

"'*Omnia Ab Uno*.' It's Latin for 'All from One.' Nobody is quite sure what it refers to, and Mr. Cage is certainly not telling. Being the optimist, I would like to think it has a biblical origin. A reminder that all creation comes from God, being the One. I'm sure there are hundreds of different opinions. I think Mr. Cage likes the mystery he has created. It's good for his image. Most actors seem to like controversy. Keeps their name in front of the public. Maybe the mystery will be revealed at the time of his death."

"I have to say, it's very strange."

"Did you know that the eccentric actor was born Nicolas Kim Coppola, nephew of *The Godfather* director Francis Ford Coppola? Mr. Cage adopted his working name to avoid nepotism and claims he got his name inspiration from Marvel superhero Luke Cage."

"I'm not familiar with Luke Cage. Can you enlighten me?"

"I can, Mr. Lancer. Luke Cage was one of the first black superheroes, appearing in American comic books published by Marvel Comics in 1972. He's an ex-convict imprisoned for a crime he didn't commit. After going through a voluntary experimental cellular-regeneration procedure, he gains superhuman strength and unbreakable skin. Once freed from prison, he becomes a superhero for hire."

"How do you remember all this?" I laugh.

"My passion for comic books, Mr. Lancer—one of my idiosyncrasies." Pointing down the row, John continues. "Just down there is the Glapion family tomb. Christophe Glapion was the domestic partner of Marie Laveau. She is believed to be in his family vault."

"Yes, I remember reading the story of her life."

"I'm going over a couple of rows toward the back, where my family vault is located. I'll meet you back at the pyramid in twenty minutes, unless you need more time."

"Thanks, John. Twenty minutes will be fine."

Finding the Glapion tomb, I make some notes and take pictures from every angle. There's a small plaque attached to the left front.

MARIE LAVEAU

**THIS GREEK REVIVAL
TOMB IS THE REPUTED
BURIAL PLACE OF THIS
NOTORIOUS "VOODOO
QUEEN". A MYSTIC CULT,
VOODOOISM, OF AFRICAN
ORIGIN, WAS BROUGHT TO
THIS CITY FROM SANTO
DOMINGO AND
FLOURISHED IN 19TH
CENTURY. MARIE LAVEAU
WAS THE MOST WIDELY
KNOWN OF MANY
PRACTISHONERS OF THE
CULT.**

Marie Laveau Tomb

Graffiti appears on the front of the vault, along with some markings of *XXX* and bobby pins. I remember the bobby pins relate to her being a hairdresser at one stage in her life. The *XXX* is for good luck and protection.

I feel a cold breeze, and the hair on my neck tingles. I turn around just in time to get a glimpse of a black women with a dark turban smile and immediately disappear. It appears to me to be Sister Moon, great-granddaughter of Marie Laveau. I rush in the direction of the apparition, but no one is there. I quickly check the adjoining rows with no luck.

Returning to the Glapion vault, I notice a red rose at the foot of the tomb, which I don't remember from just a few minutes ago. I check the pictures I took. Yes, it is there in the pictures. I check my notes. There is no mention of a rose. I can't believe I would have missed a red rose at the tomb but can't deny the pictures; it must have been there.

Heading back to the Cage pyramid, I find John waiting for me. As we return to the main gate, I hear him talking, but my mind is thinking about the last event.

"Don't you agree, Mr. Lancer?"

"I'm sorry, John. My mind was elsewhere. What were you saying?"

John stops walking and looks at me. "Are you okay, Mr. Lancer? You appear disturbed."

"Yes, John, I am. Sorry. I thought for a minute that I saw Sister Moon, but I might have been mistaken."

"Things like that happen in this cemetery. Visitors often see strange things. This place activates the imagination. The spirit world is alive and well." He smiles. "We can check with the guard at the gate. He can tell you if she was here or not."

We walk in silence until we arrive at the guardhouse. The guard comes out and makes note of our time of departure on his clipboard. "So how was your visit?" he asks.

"Very nice, sir," I reply. "This place is beautiful. I never expected to see so much ancient stonework in one place. The cemetery has done an excellent job of preserving its history."

"Thank you," the guard replies. "Is there anything else I can do for you?"

"Yes, there is," I say. "Do you know the black lady by the name of Sister Moon?"

"Well, yes and no. I know her by sight but don't know her personally. She usually comes by every two or three weeks. Why do you ask?"

"I thought I might have seen her in the cemetery. Has she been here today?"

"No, she hasn't been here today. I would have checked her in."

"You're sure about that?"

The guard gives me a queer look. "Yes, I'm very sure. I haven't left the gate since it opened this morning. There was a walking tour that came in before you arrived. Probably just someone separated from the group."

John and I thank him again for his help. We walk in silence again toward my car.

"Mr. Lancer, you're obviously disturbed by what happened. If you have time, why don't we stop over at the welcome center to get a cup of coffee? It may help to talk about it."

"Sure, John, we can do that."

We enter the center and approach the inside café. John orders a black coffee with three sugars, and I pick up a bottled water. I notice John looking in the glass case at the cannoli. I add two to our order, and we take a seat by the window.

"Mr. Lancer, sometimes our surroundings create situations in our minds that don't actually exist. It's like a dream state, wherein images from our past are comingled with the present. Like déjà vu. Images that are familiar to us are pulled together in our mind and generate another picture. That picture can be misleading and disturbing to us. Do you understand what I'm saying, Mr. Lancer?"

"Yes, John, I understand. But there is also another explanation: what I saw was real."

John takes a drink of his coffee and taps his fingers on the table. "Mr. Lancer, if we study the early philosophers, like Nostradamus and Hume, we can understand the distinction between predictions and prophecy. We all have visions or dreams at times in our lives, when we know something is going to happen or has happened. Would you consider that a prophecy or prediction?"

"The terms have been used interchangeably in the past, but to me, prophecy would have divine intervention. Anyone can predict an event in the future. Just because it comes true doesn't make the person a prophet."

John smiles and takes a bite of his cannoli. Some white powdered sugar drops onto his beard and T-shirt. Disregarding the lost fragments, he finishes the pastry in his next bite and washes it down with coffee. Half wiping his face and T-shirt with a paper napkin, he leans forward in his chair. "Let me tell you about a dream I had, Mr. Lancer. It's night, and I'm in a cemetery. There's a full moon in the sky, so I can see the silhouettes of all the headstones. The moon begins to fall to the earth. As it falls, I see the changes in its phases, going from full to crescent. The phases stop at crescent, and the residual moon appears to linger over a headstone. That's all I remember. I can't tell where this garden of stone is or see any markings on the headstone. I'm mystified by what it means. Does this mean anything to you, Mr. Lancer?"

I stare at John in disbelief. I've never mentioned anything to him about the common astrological crescent-moon tattoos of the three victims or the prediction of Sister Moon that I should be looking among the dead and not the living. I hesitate with my response.

"Mr. Lancer, are you okay? You seem distressed."

"Yes, John, I'm fine. The dream has some similar elements with the Morone case I'm involved with. Thank you for sharing it with me."

"You're welcome, Mr. Lancer. Sometimes I get premonitions, but most of the time, they don't seem to relate to anything or anybody, so I keep them to myself. I don't know why I told you about this one. Maybe because we were in the cemetery, and it was recalled to mind. I hope I didn't disturb you."

"No, John, I'm fine. Really." It takes me a minute to regain my thoughts. "Do you remember anything else about the dream? Maybe something odd in the cemetery or something in the background?"

"No, Mr. Lancer, just the cemetery headstones and the moon."

I sit in silence and stare out the window, trying to put the pieces of the puzzle together. Nothing seems to fit. There's a man in jail with no name. Three victims have a common tattoo that may or may not be related, and a suspect is on the run. Not to discount the burned-down house and school in Picayune and the new discovery that one of the victims lived in Picayune before moving to NOLA.

"Mr. Lancer?"

"I'm sorry, John. I was just trying to put all this together. I don't mean to ignore you."

"Oh, I'm fine just sitting and enjoying your company. I was wondering if you're going to eat your cannoli." He smiles.

"No, John, please help yourself." I push the dessert plate in his direction.

"Thank you, Mr. Lancer. I hate to see a good cannoli go to waste."

I watch John as he takes a bite and leans back in his chair, savoring the taste of the sweet and creamy ricotta cheese. Smiling, he salutes me as the last half disappears into his partially powdered-sugar-covered mouth.

Cleaning his face for a second time, he pats his belly. "I have to thank the island of Sicily for originating that morsel of delight. One of my favorite Italian pastries. You missed out, Mr. Lancer. There were small pieces of chocolate chips hidden inside. A surprising spike of favor that blends with the ricotta cheese."

"John, I've never heard anyone describe a cannoli quite that way." I laugh.

After some casual conversation, I find the need to separate my past thoughts and get on the road. I hope there is more to discover that will lend information to the Morone case. We walk out of the center together, and John bids me farewell and heads toward the Quarter. I retrieve my car and head to Picayune.

After a thirty-minute drive, I arrive in Picayune. Upon locating the Pine Tree Apartments, I pull into the parking lot near the office. The Pine Tree Apartments were listed on the copy of the 2017 car registration of the second victim, Mary Sadler Cotton.

Entering the office, I introduce myself to the manager and explain my need for any information that might be helpful in my investigation. Producing a copy of the registration as evidence, I inquire about the apartment listed as B6. The manager informs me he's been at this apartment location for less than a year and doesn't have knowledge of Ms. Cotton. He also indicates that each year, the records are sent to the home office in Dallas, Texas, for storage. He gives me the home office information but states that they can't give out tenant information without approval and a court order. Discouraged by the lack of information, I leave the office. My last hope is to drive around the complex to locate B6 and possibly question the occupants of the neighboring apartments without the manager noticing.

As I approach building B, I notice a man with an equipment belt examining some cracks in the sidewalk. Hoping he might be the maintenance manager, I exit my car and introduce myself to him. After a short exchange, he introduces himself as Bill Flowers. I put him around sixty years old, six foot tall, and 140 pounds. He has a slight limp and some visual damage to his left hand.

"Bill, I'm hoping you can help me with some information regarding one of your past tenants. Can you tell me how long you've been working here?"

"It'll be ten years in October. Moved here from the home office in Dallas. I had a fall in July 2008. The accident left me with some neuropathy in my left hand and a hip injury. The home office offered me a transfer to a smaller complex after the accident. I was looking for a slower pace and a place where I have some elbow room. When this came open and my wife and I visited, we fell in love with the city and its proximity to New Orleans. Property values are good, and there's plenty of farmland still available. My wife and I live here at the apartments rent free. We get small-town living with all the amenities of a big city in a thirty-minute drive."

"Sounds like a place that fits your lifestyle. May I ask you about a past tenant?"

Bill laughs. "You must have already met the apartment manager. I'm sure he turned you down. He's new at his job. Wants to do everything by the book. Depending on the question, I may be able to help you."

"Thanks, Bill. I don't know if you're aware, but early this year, a woman by the name of Mary Sadler Cotton was murdered in New Orleans. A suspect is being held at the prison. I'm gathering information for a story to be printed in the *New Orleans Chronicle*. In 2017, she lived in these apartments, in B6. I was wondering if you knew her."

"Since the lady is already dead, I don't see what harm it can do. I do have a request. If you'll assure me that my name is not mentioned in your article, I'll tell you what I know. That wouldn't go over well with management. If I don't like the question, I'll tell you. Fair enough?"

"Bill, I can promise that your name won't be mentioned. Anything you don't feel is appropriate to answer, just say so. I'm good with that. I'm just looking for background information."

"Okay. I remember Mary Cotton. She was here for a short rental. A nurse, I believe. Pretty girl. Lived by herself."

"Do you think any of her neighbors might remember her?"

"No, don't think so. This building had some settling issues after she moved out. My wife and I were living in B1, and we moved to another apartment. The other four tenants left while the renovation was going on. The tenants living in the B units now are new."

"How did you come to know her?"

"When she moved in, her apartment had a plumbing leak that I had to fix. We met then."

"Do you remember if you ever saw her with anybody? Maybe a boyfriend or someone she spent time with?"

"There was one guy I saw her with a few times. Drove a pickup truck. Don't remember what kind it was. Seems like it was dark in color. Sorry I can't be of more help. That was over a year ago."

"Do you remember what he looked like? Anything you can remember will help."

"No, not much. It's been a while. I can't really remember. Just an average joe. Nothing special."

I pull up a picture of Andre LeBlanc on my phone. "Do you think it could have been this man?"

"He doesn't look familiar, but I can't be sure."

I move over to a picture of Raymond Morone. "What about this guy? Does he look familiar?"

"You know, I really can't remember. Sorry."

"The pickup truck you saw—did it look like a work truck? Maybe had some tools or supplies in the bed?"

"Yeah, I'd say it was a work truck. I saw a welding torch in the bed and asked if he did handrail welding. He said he'd get back with me. That didn't make a lot of sense. Either you do or you don't. Pretty expensive tool to be leaving in an open bed. I never saw him again after that."

"Do you remember anybody by the name of Raymond Morone or Andre LeBlanc? Those names mean anything to you?"

"No, can't say they do."

"Thanks, Bill." Handing him my card, I continue. "If anything else comes to mind, please give a call."

"I will," he replies.

After exiting the apartment complex, I head over to the Picayune Memorial Gardens. After parking outside the gate, I walk down the last road near the left side of the stainless-steel chain-link fence. The garden is well manicured, and the aroma of fresh flowers accompanies the gentle wind. Cherub statues stand and sit alongside many of the graves, protecting family members who are no longer among the living. Vaults are adorned with crosses casting shadows upon the hallowed ground. Carved flowers and lambs encircle many of the names and dates of the deceased.

Bill Tamboli's grave is located on this side, near the back. Within a few minutes, I arrive at his headstone. The inscription on the headstone reads, "The Shepherd calls his sheep, and they know His voice. William James Tamboli. Born February 12, 1981. Died June 30, 1999. Son of John William and Alice Sales Tamboli."

The damage on the left side of the headstone is a cut into its concrete, probably from a chisel. The cut is lighter than the surrounding area and must have been done later than the original headstone. The cut is an X. I circle the headstone to get a look at its back. No other marks are present.

Still thinking about John's dream and how or if it relates to this case, I find myself wandering around the cemetery, looking for a crescent moon or another X on any of the graves. After a thirty-minute stroll, I admit defeat and leave.

My next stop is the overgrown lot with the burned-down house on Route 43. I want to get a closer look at the brush pile and the rectangular enclosure that appeared on Google Earth.

After pulling into the lot, I exchange my shoes for a pair of army boots. Walking along the destroyed block foundation of the house, I see that little is left, except the remnants of a brick chimney. Moving through the overgrown lot toward the pond area, I approach the brush pile for examination. The pile appears to be composed mostly of tree branches and common house trash. Scattered among the trash are burned wood, some pieces of furniture, parts of light fixtures, broken porcelain, and bedsprings. This pile would have been made from a bulldozer after the burned remains of the house were discarded. I poke around in the trash but discover nothing of interest.

Walking another twenty yards, I come upon the wood enclosure. The top of the enclosure is slanted for water runoff and has rotted over the years. A visible pump is inside. The rusted hinges that once held a useful door are intact. On the remaining piece, there's a heart carved into the wood with the initials *BT + DC*. I assume the *BT* is Bill Tamboli and the *DC* is an early girlfriend. At the other end of the partial door is an *X*, with a dark black stain at the top and bottom of the *X*. Both marks appear to have been made many years ago, since they conform to the rotting wood. I spend a lot of time examining every aspect of the pump enclosure, inside and out. Nothing else is found. Taking a break to clear my mind, I take a walk along the pond's edge.

A gentle wind breathes through a willow tree as its long, spiny fingers dangle over the water's edge. The calm brownish water lies still until interrupted by a falling leaf that floats down from above. Surrounding the attacker, small circles appear, dissipating in a few seconds. Looking across the pond, I see the tree-lined edge mirrored on the water's surface, confusing the mind of its reality. Hidden in the tall grass, I find a couple of deteriorated cane poles. As if trying to maintain a memory of their past life, they struggle to hold a piece of fishing line and cork float. Near them, several rusted coffee cans, half covered by dirt and grass, remain as a sign of the expedition that took place.

As the landscape closes in on the pond's edge, my advance becomes blocked. Upon returning to my car, I change my shoes and decide to pay another visit to Mr. Bo Watkins.

I find Mr. Watkins sitting on the front porch, in his favorite chair with ole Jake. As I approach, Jake lifts his head, takes a sniff, and looks over at Mr. Watkins.

"It's okay, Jake. Just that young man who was here the other day,"

Bo says, and Jake appears to nod in agreement and returns to his restful posture.

"Hello, Mr. Watkins. Do you remember me?"

"Hell, boy, you were just here yesterday. I'm old, but my mind isn't dead yet." He laughs.

"No, I guess not," I reply. Staying at the bottom of the stairs so as not to infringe on ole Jake's territory, I continue. "I meant to ask you yesterday if you remember another boy living at the Tamboli house. Thought you might have seen someone else staying there."

Bo Watkins takes a drink of tea from a mason jar and pulls on his earlobe, as if pondering the question. "You know, I do remember seeing a couple of boys playing in the front yard on occasion when I drove by. Throwing a baseball or football back and forth. Don't know if he was living there or not."

"But you don't remember who this boy was?"

"No, just a couple of kids playing in the yard. Didn't pay much attention to who it was. I try to mind my own business, if you know what I mean." He smiles.

"Who you talking to?" a voice asks from inside the screen door.

"Just that young man who was here yesterday!" Bo yells. "What's your name again?"

"Justin. Justin Lancer," I reply.

The door opens, and an elderly lady steps out onto the porch. She could be the sister of Aunt Bee from *The Andy Griffith Show*. She has the same silver hair and blue-flowered dress. She's holding a mason jar of tea. "Brought you a glass of tea." She smiles, moving to the top of the steps, and hands it down.

"Thank you, Mrs. Watkins. I can really use this."

"So what brings you back to our neck of the woods?" she asks.

"I was just following up with your husband about the Tamboli family. I have reason to believe there may have been another boy who stayed with them. Mr. Watkins said he remembers a couple of boys playing ball in the front yard but isn't sure if the other boy lived there."

"No, can't say I know either. The family didn't socialize much.

I never saw them at church or other town gatherings. Stayed to themselves."

Finishing my tea, I hand the jar back to Mrs. Watkins. "Thank you for the tea. It hit the spot."

Mrs. Watkins smiles and disappears back into the abyss.

"Mr. Watkins, do you remember if the Tamboli boy played any sports?"

"No, can't say I do. Don't remember him written up in the local paper, if that's what you mean."

"Well, I have to thank you again. You have been helpful."

"Come back anytime. Me and ole Jake like to talk about old times. Ain't that right, Jake?"

Ole Jake raises his head, and I swear he laughs.

"Besides, your first two trips are free. Any more answers, and I'll have to start charging for them. Man's got to make a living." Bo smiles.

"I'll keep that in mind. Thanks again."

Before leaving town, I pull into the parking lot of Margaret Reed Cosby Memorial Library and enter the building. After heading to the reference section, I pull the high school yearbooks from 1997, 1998, 2000, and 2001. My hope is to find someone with the initials *DC*.

Nothing matches. If DC attended Picayune High School, she could be listed in 1999, the year of the missing book.

On my way home, I get a call from Kate. She tells me her flight from Hawaii will arrive in New Orleans at 7:15 a.m. after a red-eye transfer through LAX. I agree to pick her up at Louis Armstrong Airport. She apologizes for the short notice but informs me she has an interview at Tulane the following day. She seems excited about a possible change in her lifestyle, and so am I. The thought of picking up our relationship has me spellbound.

As I arrive back in NOLA, my thoughts are torn as I struggle with a decision to visit my old friend Viper. I decide to stop in at the Cave later tonight. My questions will be about his knowledge of Andre LeBlanc.

CHAPTER 8

I arrive at the Cave at eleven forty-five. As I pull into the parking lot, I see Viper and his nest of snakes enter the side door. I count five in all. Once they are inside, I turn my headlights back on to get a better view of the parking area. I see five pickup trucks, two cars, and two choppers. The tags I can see are registered in Louisiana. I wait a few minutes so as not to expose myself too soon. Out of instinct, I pat my cargo pants pocket to ensure I have my Kel-Tec .380.

As I enter, Matt the bartender is placing a round of beers on the counter. Looking up, he shakes his head, mumbles something under his breath, and disappears with the beers out the back door.

Casing the inside, I count twelve people. Two are at the pool table, while the others are seated at tables. There is an even distribution of men and women, and the largest group is four. All are talking or laughing and take little notice of my entrance. The couple at the pool table are playing kissy-face and don't seem to care much about their game. The table of four appear to be the motorcycle group. A bearded man at the table sports motorcycle boots and a red bandanna do-rag. His dark red beard is tied at the bottom, pulled into a point. I take special notice of a knife and scabbard strapped onto his boot. The speakers are blaring "Screaming Night Hog," an early 1970s hit by Steppenwolf. I stand at the bar counter until Matt comes back.

"What ya drinking?" Matt asks.

"Bud in a bottle," I reply. "Make that two."

"Five bucks."

I place a ten-dollar bill on the counter. "Keep the change."

Matt picks up the money but gives no reply.

"Tell Viper Justin Lancer is here and would like to talk with him."

"Tell 'im yourself. I'm busy." He smiles.

Taking my beer along, I walk out the back door. The area is lined with a wood fence and gate. Plastic tables and chairs occupy the interior. Small strings of lights hang overhead. The smell of marijuana permeates the air. Two goth men stand up from their chairs. Viper looks up to see who has invaded his den. Recognizing me, he raises his hand and motions for his brood to relax.

"You're disturbing our meeting. And you were not invited. I suggest you leave now."

"I'll leave when I'm through," I say. I pull up a chair, place it across from Viper, and place one of the beers in front of him. "Tell your goons to get lost so we can have a nice, pleasant conversation. A couple of questions, and I'm out of here."

Viper smiles and waves off his companions. They leave the area through the gate. He accepts the beer and takes a drink. As he leans back in his chair, the overhead lights reflect off his painted white face and green snake eyes.

"I'm looking for a tattoo artist by the name of Andre LeBlanc. He worked at Carnal Ink."

"And what makes you think I know him?"

"The tattoo on your neck. It had to be done by an exceptional artist. I've been told LeBlanc is the best in NOLA. That true?"

Viper takes a slow drink of beer. His black-painted lips force a smile. "That's true."

"Where can I find him?"

"Heard he's on the run. The only person who might know is his cousin Willy. Check with him."

"Do you know of anyone he might be staying with? Maybe a girlfriend?"

"As I said, check with Willy."

Figuring the conversation is over, I pick up my beer and return to the bar area. Three of Viper's goons are inside. Two are standing at the counter, one on each end, and the other one is by the side door. Matt is nowhere to be found. As I walk toward the door, the snake at the far end steps in my way. In the glass reflection behind the bar, I notice the other one steps out behind my back.

"If you want to leave here in one piece, you'd better step out of my way. Not a warning but a promise." I stand my ground to brace myself for their next move.

In the next second, the two motorcycle guys appear. The bearded man with the do-rag steps between me and my confronter. The other man slides in behind my back.

The bearded man leans on the counter and starts a calm conversation. "I wonder where Matt is. My buddy and me need a beer." He turns to the goth man in front of him. "Why don't you three guys get behind the counter and get us three beers? I did say three, didn't I? Just wanted to be sure you heard me right. You know, if there's anything I hate, it is somebody being outnumbered. Especially a nice young man like this. Reminds me of a bunch of bullies. I don't like bullies. I don't know if anyone told you, but Mardi Gras is over, so you can turn in your costume. This was a nice place until you thugs started showing up. I suggest you get those beers and move your ass out of this man's way. I'm tired of looking at you."

The snake signals to his companions, and they back off, stepping aside. They start toward the back door.

"Hey, what about our beers?" the biker yells.

"Get your own beers."

"Well, that's not being very neighborly." He laughs. Extending his hand, he introduces himself. "Name's Jeff. Fellow who had your back is Jim. Hope you don't mind us stepping in, but those freaks really piss me off. When I saw them gathering in here, I knew something was about to come down. You look like you could have handled the situation by yourself, but there was no way I was going to let those baboons get the upper hand."

"My name's Justin. I appreciate you guys stepping up. It never hurts to have backup."

"I know who you are. We have a mutual colleague."

"Who might that be?" I ask.

"Dominic. He asked me to look out for you whenever I was here. I come here about once a month to check on the snake pit."

"You have me at a disadvantage. Can you elaborate a little more?"

Suddenly, Matt appears again.

"Let's step outside a minute. I don't trust Casper," Jeff says, motioning his head at Matt. Turning to his friend Jim, Jeff continues. "Look after the ladies for a minute. I'm stepping outside to get some fresh air."

Jim nods and moves back to their table.

Outside the building, Jeff takes a tobacco pouch from his pocket and presses it between the teeth and lower lip. He's six foot two and around 250 pounds. Under the side-door light, I can see a large, crinkly scar on his left arm, which could be from a massive burn. On his forearm I recognize a tattoo: an arrowhead with a bayonet and three lightning bolts, the mark of Army Airborne Special Forces, often called the Green Berets.

"So you seem to already know about me from Dominic. Can you tell me how you fit in all this?" I ask.

"I run an undercover drug operation for the department. I've been watching Viper and his band of snakes for a while now. So far, nothing hard has been coming in. Just some pot and hash. The word's out on the street that Detective DeAngelis has been by here. I know most of the dealers in the area by sight, and they're staying clear."

"That all makes more sense now. Thanks for letting me know. I hope this incident didn't blow your chances of getting closer to Viper. I don't think those guys inside will be welcoming you with open arms."

"Nah, not a chance. If Viper starts dealing in heavy stuff, he'll be looking for a hardnose. Viper is a small fry. Those freaks of his don't have the guts to play with the big boys. You can't take a bunch of clowns and expect to get anything more than a bunch of clowns. Viper is smart enough to know that. I'd say my chances are rather good." He smiles.

"I notice by your tattoo that you were in Special Forces. If I'd seen that inside, I would have just taken a seat and enjoyed the action." I laugh.

Jeff smiles. "That was a long time ago, but I'm still up for duty when the call comes. Reaction time is slower, but I'm sure I can still snap a few necks. I'm only glad I didn't have to exert myself. These old bones are a little rusty."

"Well, I appreciate your help. By the way, did Dominic inform you about the tattoo artist Andre LeBlanc? I have a feeling he might show up here."

"Yes, I'll keep my eyes open for him."

"Thanks again. I'm going to head home and put this body to bed. Got a long day tomorrow. Call me if I can help you." I hand him my card, and we separate and go our own ways.

By the time I arrive home, it's 1:40 a.m. I make some coffee and sit down to finish an article I've started for the *Chronicle*. Following my prior themes, I put together the last two pages on the cemeteries of New Orleans and the haunted ghost tours, some of NOLA's popular tourist attractions. After several rewrites and editing, I push the Send button.

After refilling my cup, I step out the back door and relax at the picnic table. A slight breeze paces itself across the patio. The lights from inside cast shadows along the back fence. I can see the silhouette of honeysuckle vines and their small, tubular flowers that drape the fence's face. Their fragrance is sweet and intoxicating. The silence is eerie yet calming.

I close the cluttered drawers of my mind, and my thoughts turn to Kate. The times when we've laughed and the times when we've cried. The silly movies she loves and her favorite restaurants. Picnics in City Park and walks along the river. Evenings when we sat at this very table and talked for hours about work, poetry, books, TV, or world affairs. The subject was not as important as the sharing of hearts. I want things to be like they were but wonder if time has changed our destiny.

The spell is broken by the hoot of a barn owl. Smiling, I drink the last sip of coffee and go back inside to get a couple hours of sleep before I meet Kate.

After tossing restlessly for an hour, I shower, shave, and make a new pot of joe. After throwing some bread into the toaster, I open my computer to get some research done before I leave. The new information on Bill Tamboli's parents from the cemetery might help. With his dad's middle name and his mother's maiden name, I can do a deeper search than before. With this information, I easily find Bill's birth and death certificates. All the dates and names agree with what I already have. Pulling up their census from 1990, I see that Bill is the only child listed, age nine. Their place of residence was Hammond, Louisiana. In 2000, after Bill's death, his parents were living in Mobile, Alabama. By 2010, I find Bill's dad listed as residing in Orange County, California.

Searching marriage and divorce information on both parents, I find that Bill's parents divorced in 2004. Bill's mother, Alice Sales Tamboli, remarried in 2008 to Richard Paul Lane of Hammond, Louisiana.

Checking the time, I reluctantly set aside this information for later. If Bill's mother is still living, which I believe she is, this could be the opening I've been hoping for. If Bill's high school best friend was indeed Raymond Morone, Alice Sales Lane could hold a major missing piece of the puzzle.

After rushing out the door, I head to Louis Armstrong International Airport in Kenner. As I pull into the arrivals lane, I spot Kate waiting at the curb with her cell phone in hand. I get an incoming call.

"I see you, Kate. I'm about four cars back. Be there shortly."

"Okay, thanks," she replies.

After throwing her carry-on bag into the back, I get a short kiss and hug. "I'm so glad you're home. I really missed you. How was your flight?"

"Grueling, to say the least. LAX was a nightmare. I thought I'd miss my connection, but I made it just in time. My bags will be in on the next flight. I've arranged for a driver to deliver them."

"So tell me about your interview. Are you considering a lifestyle change?"

"I'm excited about the opportunity. Travel has gotten stressful, and the photo shoots are more demanding. I miss seeing my parents, you, and all my friends. If the position pans out, I'd strongly consider the change."

As we pull onto I-10 toward Metairie, a hundred questions flush my mind. It's hard to believe that after all these years, Kate and I may have an opportunity to share our life together.

"Tell me about the call. Where did the interview come from?"

"When I was working on my graduate degree in Chicago, I became friends with the dean in the department of arts. She left the institute after my graduation, and we lost track of each other. She called me in Hawaii and reconnected. She said she had found me on Facebook and done some further research on my portfolio listed on my website. She finished her doctorate degree in fine arts and is the director of arts at Tulane. I'm excited to see her again after all these years. She set up the interview with the president of Tulane and three members of the board of trustees. I have my interview at four o'clock."

After pulling into Kate's driveway, I grab her carry-on and walk her to her door. "You'd better get a quick nap. You have a busy day ahead."

"I've got too much to do. Besides, there's no way I could sleep."

"Do you feel like getting together later tonight after your interview? I'd love to hear all about it. How about a quick dinner? I can pick up some soup and sandwiches at Panera and meet you back here at seven. I know you're tired, and I need to get back home early myself."

"Yes, I'd like that."

I get my second hug and kiss. "See you at seven. Call me if anything changes."

As soon as I arrive back home, I heat up the coffee and dive back into the information on Bill Tamboli's mother. Alice's second husband died of cancer in 2015. I find their residence that year listed on the death certificate as 190 Scale Road in Hammond, Louisiana. Exploring the current residence in Hammond from their directory, I find Alice Lane is still listed at the Scale Road address. I make note of her phone number and set it aside for a later call.

I go to the Hammond City website and print off a copy of the city map and the address of the main library in case I need it. Hammond is the largest city in Tangipahoa Parish, Louisiana. Located forty-five miles northwest of New Orleans, it had a population of 20,019 in 2010.

I also run a background check on Bill Flowers, the maintenance manager at the Pine Tree Apartments in Picayune. His background is clear, and he lived in Dallas until 2008, before moving to Mississippi, as he stated. Nothing here throws up a red flag.

Running my ancestry program on Alice Sales, I find her birth records. Alice Marie Sales was born on August 16, 1952, in Hammond, Louisiana. Her parents were Edwin Joseph Sales and Francis Elizabeth Barlow. Cross-checking with the census information of 1970, I find Alice is listed as the younger of two sisters. The older sister, Margaret Francis Sales, was nineteen years old in 1970, and Alice was eighteen.

At ten o'clock that morning, I place a call to the number I've found for Alice Lane. I get her answering machine and leave a message. In the short time, I explain the best I can who I am and what I'm calling about. After I hang up, I don't feel good about the message I've left. Writing out another script, I decide to place another call later today if I haven't heard back from her.

While refreshing my coffee, I get a call on my cell phone from Cindy, our receptionist at the *Chronicle*. Her message is short, and I can hear Rocco's voice in the background. She relays the message that

Rocco wants me to stop by the office today. I tell her I can be there within the hour. After tidying up the kitchen table, I gather up my notes, close my computer, and head to the office.

When I enter the *Chronicle* office, Cindy waves me into Rocco's office. The smell of stale cigar smoke welcomes me. Chewing on a Parodi cigarillo, Rocco looks up and motions for me to take a seat. He's wearing a flowered shirt with a missing button. His hair is wild and sticking out over his ears. On his desk are a mess of papers, two coffee cups, and a can of Mountain Dew. His ashtray is full of ashes and cigarillo butts.

"Where the hell is my Morone story? It's been almost three weeks, and I've seen nothing!" he yells.

Remaining calm, I go through all the work I've been doing on the story. I explain to him the detailed research and the travel back and forth to Picayune. I cover the information on the Tamboli house and my belief that Morone is lying about his name and background. We talk about Andre Leblanc and his relationship to Morone and the victims. I show him the information I've assembled and explain that Bill Tamboli's mother is still living and resides in Hammond. I tell him I've called her and left a message, but she hasn't returned my call. I try to impress on him that through her, I may have a real chance of finding the needed information on Morone. So far, nothing Morone has told me can be verified.

The whole time I'm talking, Rocco is fumbling with papers and taking notes. When I finish, Rocco leans back in his chair and yells at Cindy. When Cindy enters his office, he orders her to call Mayor Phil Black in Hammond and put the call through to his phone.

Rocco asks a few more questions about Bill Tamboli and Morone. After several more minutes of discussion, Rocco yells at Cindy again. "Where's my phone call? Did you get the mayor's office?"

"Yes!" Cindy yells back. "His secretary said he was busy and took our number. Said she would give him the message."

"Did you give her my name?"

"I told her it was the *New Orleans Chronicle*."

"Call her back! That woman is a ditz! Tell her it's Rocco Donalli.

She doesn't know the *Chronicle* from the *Wall Street Journal*. Tell her I need to talk to Phil right away."

"Yes, sir."

Feeling irritated with Rocco's interference, I speak up. "You don't need to get involved. I can handle this."

Holding up his hand to stop my conversation, Rocco nips back. "I'm sure you can, but I need to get this thing moving. Watch and learn, grasshopper."

Rocco's phone rings. He smiles at me and picks up. "Phil, how are things in Hammond?" After a short delay, he continues. "I'm going to put you on speaker. I have my ace reporter here with me, and we could use your help." As he pushes the speaker button, the mayor responds.

"That's fine. What can I help you with?"

"There's a widow living in Hammond we desperately need to speak with concerning a friend of her family. She hasn't responded to our calls. With her not knowing us from Adam, I can understand that. If you could introduce us to her, it would go a long way in getting the interview."

"I don't see any issue with that. What's her name?"

Rocco looks up at me for the answer.

"Alice Lane," I reply. "She lives on Wood Scale Road, off Highway 190."

The mayor laughs before continuing. "Not only do I know Alice, but she worked here at the courthouse for several years. She retired a year ago. I'll be glad to call her and let you know when you can follow up. It'll be next week, though. I ran into her and her sister last week at Walmart, and they were going on an Alaskan cruise. They won't be back until then. What's your reporter's name?"

"Justin Lancer."

"Got it. I'll let you know as soon as I get hold of Alice."

"Thanks, Phil. I really appreciate your help," Rocco replies.

"You coming to our annual dove shoot this year?" the mayor asks.

"Count me in. I'll bring the steaks."

"Great. Looking forward to seeing you."

Hanging up his phone, Rocco smiles and directs his attention to me. "I expect a draft of your article by the end of next week. Now, get out of here, and get some work done."

Holding back my anger, I get up and leave without comment.

I stop at the first Starbucks I see and order a Caffè Misto at the counter and take a seat. I stare at the coffee and wonder why I even ordered it. I've had more than enough coffee for one day. My irritation with Rocco for his interference has left a knot in my craw. Reliving our conversation, I must admit the outcome was a favorable result. What burns me is his condescending manner. Maybe what's bothering me is his arrogance. Or could it be my own? Either way, my investigation is moving forward.

I love what I do but don't appreciate being pushed around by a bully. I understand leadership and control from my days in the army, but in my mind, Rocco overextends his authority. I realize for the first time why I choose not to work out of the office anymore. It has to do with his overbearing and inimical attitude. I know one thing: I need to put all my effort into the Morone case and worry about my relationship with Rocco and the *Chronicle* later.

Putting aside my feelings, I give Dominic a call to update him on my latest information and see if he has had any luck in finding LeBlanc. He informs me that he is on Esplanade Avenue, over by City Park. He says he can meet me for a po'boy at the Parkway Bakery and Tavern on Hagan Street in the Bayou St. John neighborhood.

When I pull into the parking lot, Dominic is standing outside, talking on his phone. As I approach, he hangs up and opens the entry door.

"You been here before?" he asks.

"Not in a long time."

"In my estimate, they have the best po'boys in NOLA. Fresh local oysters on Monday and Wednesday and shrimp right out of the Gulf."

"Sounds good. I'm hungry."

"You won't be disappointed."

At the counter, Dominic orders the James Brown Special: fried shrimp, brisket, and pepper jack cheese smothered in barbecue sauce and topped with lettuce, tomatoes, pickles, onions, and peppers. I order their roast beef special dressed, soaked in brown gravy. After grabbing a couple of drinks, we pick a table near the back where we can talk.

While we eat, I bring Dominic up to date on meeting with Viper and running into Jeff, the undercover agent, at the Cave. I cover my last trip to Picayune and the opportunity to meet with Bill Tamboli's mother later. Dominic listens attentively but seems unimpressed with the information.

Not getting a response, I ask about LeBlanc. "Anything new on LeBlanc?"

"No, nothing for now. We're still tracking his cousin Willy, but he's staying clear of LeBlanc. Sooner or later, he'll screw up, and we'll get the information we need. I went by his work the other day and put some more pressure on him. He got all tongue-tied and repeated himself several times. We're going to watch him for another week, and if nothing happens, I'll pull him in for questioning. I think that'll shake him up enough to show his hand."

"What can you tell me about the third victim?"

"Name was Teresa Elaine McCall. Thirty-six. Worked at the minimarket by the airport. She was found March 13 at the Webster Apartments on Carrollton. She had worked the three-to-eleven shift. She clocked out at the regular time and headed home. Either she was followed, or somebody was waiting for her at the apartment. Time of death was around midnight. She lived by herself and moved here from Meridian, Mississippi. Hadn't been in town but four months."

"I spoke with the coroner's office after the autopsy. Their thought was that she was strangled from outside the car window, whereas the first two murders appear to have happened inside their cars. Do you agree with their conclusion?"

"Yes, the rope-burn marks on her neck and the damage to the steering wheel were consistent with that. If you're implying the victim might not have known her assailant, that doesn't necessarily follow."

"I agree, but if the murderer was in her car and then got out and went around to the driver's side, he or she would have had to put on gloves while walking around. The murderer wouldn't have had gloves on while sitting inside the car. Since there were no prints inside the car, the only conclusion is that she knew the assailant. Why else would she roll down her window at midnight?"

"Yes, I agree with that."

"I was also told that she had two recent tattoos. The coroner's office estimated they were done within the last three months. So it's very possible they were done here in NOLA. Were you able to get any information from the video camera at Carnal Ink?"

"No, nothing. They tape over their video every week to save money."

"Are there any street cameras that could help?"

"There're two in that area, but neither one shows Carnal Ink's entry. I'll let you know when I follow up with Willy. Call me if you get any new information from the Tamboli woman. I still think you're wasting your time. Even if you find out Morone's real name, it doesn't change anything."

"Maybe, maybe not. What I'm looking for is a motive. Without that, a jury won't convict anyone."

"Motive! Let me tell you about motive. When you've been on the street for as long as I have, you stop caring about motive. I've seen people killed over a beer, a dart game, or a parking space. My job is to find them and get them off the street. I let the lawyers and judges worry about motive. Let them play their silly game." Dominic leans in to get my attention. "You're a good investigator. I'd put you up there with most of the detectives in the department. But you're naive. There's no way Morone will get off by some technicality. Not a chance. We have too much evidence. Morone will burn, and probably his sidekick LeBlanc will along with him."

I stare at Dominic for a few seconds. I know I should be insulted, but I find myself starting to laugh. Dominic looks around and gives me a queer look.

"You're the second person today to call me naive. Maybe I am, but I know that when people become invisible, they lose hope."

Dominic remains silent, maybe pondering my statement.

Knowing I'm probably not going to change his mind, I switch the subject. I rave about the po'boy and his luncheon pick. "That homemade banana pudding looked really good. How about a cup?"

"Sure." Dominic beams. "Always ready for some 'nana pudding."

After finishing our dessert, we talk a little about NOLA and the Mardi Gras that ended in February. Dominic explains that the French *Mardi Gras*, literally translated, means "Fat Tuesday." The second murder took place just two days before Fat Tuesday, on February 11. The Mardi Gras celebration normally takes place two weeks before Fat Tuesday and ends that Tuesday at midnight. The following day, Ash Wednesday, is the beginning of the Lenten season. Fat Tuesday, called Shrove Tuesday by many Christians, makes a special point of self-examination, repentance, and amendments for spiritual growth. The name Shrove Tuesday comes from the word *shrive*, meaning "absolve." New Orleans has an attendance of more than a million people for the Mardi Gras celebration.

"Did you eat some king cake this year?" I ask.

"Yes, I did. We had a cake at the department. I got the baby." He laughs. "Now I have to bring the cake next year."

I remember my mom telling me about the cake and the baby when I lived at home. The king cake is an oval-shaped cake that's a cross between a coffee cake and a French pastry. It was brought to NOLA from France in 1870. The baby originally represented the baby Jesus and was eaten on January 6, the Feast of the Epiphany, which marks the arrival of the three wise men. Over the years, the baby evolved into a more secular symbol of good luck and prosperity. The baby is inserted into the cake, and whoever gets the piece with the baby in it brings the king cake the following year or throws the next Mardi Gras party. There are more than 750,000 king cakes sold every year.

"Mardi Gras was as crazy as ever," Dominic says. "Every year, it gets more tourists. I think I heard the number was 1.4 million. When you throw that many people together with booze and drugs, bad things happen. Three people were fatally shot, and several others were injured in three separate shootings. There was a woman hit and killed by a float. The crowd said she was reaching for some beads. A trinket—a bunch of plastic beads on a piece of string. What has this world come to?"

"The *Chronicle* always covers the celebration. It's their biggest two weeks of circulation. There's always plenty to write about."

Dominic and I talk awhile longer before heading to our cars. I need to get home to start putting together a second draft of the Morone article. I'll send Rocco something next week to keep him satisfied, if that is possible. I believe it could take another two weeks before I finish my investigation. There are too many open ends.

I get a text from Kate at 6:10 p.m. She says she's finished with the interview and has a dinner engagement with the director tomorrow night. She says she will run by the grocery store and will be home by seven.

After finishing some editing, I set aside the article and head to Panera Bread to pick up some soup and sandwiches. Kate always orders their broccoli cheddar soup and chipotle chicken avocado sandwich. Pulling through the drive-through, I pick up two of each. When I arrive at Kate's, she's already home and watching through the glass door.

"Hi, babe." Kate greets me with a kiss. "I'm starving. I haven't eaten since lunch. What'd you bring me?"

"Your favorite."

"You're the best. Set it on the table. What do you want to drink? I picked up some California zinfandel on the way home."

"Perfect. Half glass for me and some water will be great."

After giving me another hug, she sits down. "I'm so glad to be home."

Looking at her, I feel smitten all over again. Her short auburn hair, green eyes, and petite frame envelop me. "I'm glad you're back too. I miss you more every time you leave. So tell me about your interview. The suspense is killing me."

"It went extremely well. Three members of the board of trustees, the president, and the director of arts were there. I brought my photos from Hawaii so they could see what I've been doing for *National Geographic*. They all raved over the photos from around the volcano. They all had copies of my background that the director had handed out but asked many more questions. I think they were more concerned with my professionalism and presentation than my credentials. We talked about my travel. If I continued to pursue magazine photography, it would be restricted during the school term."

"That's a big change in your lifestyle. How did you handle that?"

"I can't believe I said this, but I told them I have been considering that change for some time. When I said it out loud, it confirmed how I really feel. I would like to make that change."

"Kate, that would be fantastic. You know how I feel about you. I want nothing more than to spend our time together. But it must be what is right for you."

"I've been thinking about it a lot lately. I'm going to talk to the director more tomorrow night. I could still do some shoots locally and even have my students participate. That would give them a sense of what it would be like if they wanted to pursue that career. It would also give them contacts after graduation and expand their talents. If the director agrees with me, I'm going to accept their offer."

"I'm speechless. It's a dream come true."

"Enough about me. Tell me—how's your investigation going?"

"It's been stressful, to say the least. I think I told you that the man in jail goes by the name Raymond Morone."

"You don't think that's his real name?"

"No, I'm sure it's not. From all the information I've gathered, I'm led to believe he has taken this name as a cover-up. What he's covering up I'm not sure yet. I finally tracked down his high school friend's mother in Hammond. Although I'm still not entirely convinced his high school friend was really his high school friend. He might be made up too. It's been a real roller coaster. Rocco has been pushing me to get a story ready for printing. I don't feel right about putting together a story that lacks all the information."

"Didn't you tell me once that Rocco sometimes changes your article in order to sell more papers?"

"Yes, that's true. It used to be minor changes, but lately, they've gotten more significant. It bothers me more now than it used to."

"I'm sure you'll do the right thing. Maybe it's time for a job change."

The statement hits me between the eyes. "I love what I do. I can't imagine doing anything else."

"Maybe it's not what you do but whom you do it for. There're a lot of papers who would love to have your talent. You don't have to work for a tabloid."

"That's what I love about you: brains and beauty."

"What's your plan for tomorrow?" Kate asks.

"I was thinking about going to see my parents. I haven't been by in a while."

"Great minds think alike." She laughs. "I need to run by and see mine too. They're expecting me around lunchtime. I still have to get some of my thoughts together for tomorrow night."

"You seem truly excited about this job offer."

"I really am. It'll be a big change in my life, but I think I'm ready. The idea of helping to develop a program that could bring together classroom study and the outside business world is attractive. There's a need for good journalists and photographers today. So much is computer-generated. Give me my Kodachrome, and I'll conquer the world." She laughs.

"Whatever happened to the old Kodachrome film?"

"With the advancements of digital photography in 2000, the demand for all film declined. In 2009, Kodak announced it would no longer manufacture Kodachrome film. In 2010, the last roll of Kodachrome manufactured was developed for Steve McCurry, a *National Geographic* photographer. McCurry had asked Kodak for the last roll in stock and then gone out on his own to use that roll. Although McCurry retains ownership of the slides, prints of the thirty-six slides are permanently housed at the George Eastman House in New York.

Most of the pictures were published on the internet by *Vanity Fair* magazine."

Kate talks a little more about her work and the trip to Hawaii. She shows me some of her pictures of Kilauea and the island waterfalls. From the helicopter, she took shots of molten lava spewing into the air, the kind of shots that would generate high interest at the International Photography Awards in New York.

"These are outstanding. Do you think *National Geographic* will consider putting these in the award show in New York?"

"I hope so. I think this is some of my best work."

We talk a little more, and I can tell Kate is fading. "I know you're tired and have another big day tomorrow. I'm going to head home. Call me tomorrow after your dinner."

"I will." She laughs. "My body is still in jet lag."

We walk to the door, where I get my good-night kiss. "Have I told you lately that I love you?" I ask.

"Yes, but I love to hear it again. Love you too, babe."

On my way home, I call my dad and set up a trip for tomorrow to Baton Rouge. I want to speak with him and Mom about Kate and my job situation. Dad was a pharmacist, and Mom finished her PhD in psychology at Tulane and taught there until retirement. Both retired after they sold their property at the lake and moved to Baton Rouge. Mom can give me some guidance into someone taking on another identity. There could be some underlying mental condition that contributes to a cover-up. I also want to run by the apartment and workplace of the third victim. Maybe I can find another piece of the puzzle.

CHAPTER 9

I arrive at my parents' house at nine o'clock in the morning. When I enter the backyard gate, Dad is sitting under the covered backyard patio with a cup of coffee. Two flowerpots hang from the patio rafters. Water spots below them give up their secret of being freshly nourished. The yard is immaculate. Yellow rosebushes in full bloom line the back—my mom's favorite color. White and pink azaleas are being pampered by an occasional bee. A dark green hummingbird hovers over a tubular red feeder, sizing up the sweet red liquid that begs for a consumer.

"Hi, Dad."

"Hey, Justin. Good to see you. Your mom was excited when I told her you'd be dropping by. How was your trip?"

"Very nice. You never know about morning traffic in New Orleans. Today was perfect—no issues."

"I know what you mean. I don't miss rush hour one bit. Retirement has been a blessing. I get up when I want, do whatever I like, and go to bed when I feel like it—if, of course, it meets with your mother's approval." He laughs. "Coffee on the table." He motions to a table along the side of the house wall. A Keurig coffee maker and mixed ingredients possess most of the table. "Mom will be out in a minute. She has to look exactly right for her only son."

"Believe I will."

As the coffee maker starts its process, Mom appears through the back door. "I thought I heard you two boys talking." Giving me a big hug, she takes my hand. "Don't stay away so long. You know we miss seeing you."

"I know, Mom. I'll do better. I promise."

As we take our seats, I feel a little ashamed that I haven't come over more often. Dad looks older. His hair appears thinner than I remember. I notice a few more spots on his forehead. I can tell he's lost some weight. His T-shirt fits more loosely, and his shorts appear baggy. His legs reveal an apparent loss of calf-muscle definition.

Mom never seems to age. She looks like she did ten years ago. Her petite frame and short hair remind me of Kate. She has the same green eyes but with silver hair, and there's not a wrinkle or spot on her face.

"What's been going on with your life?" Dad asks.

"I've been really busy with a case I wanted to talk to Mom about. But one of the main reasons I wanted to talk to you both is to let you know that Kate is back in town."

"That's wonderful news," my mom says. "You two have something to tell us?" She grins.

"She has a job offer at Tulane to head up the photography department. She says she would like to get off the road and is considering taking the job."

"When will she know for sure?" my dad asks.

"She's meeting with the department director tonight. If they come to an understanding, I think she'll accept."

"Oh, Justin, I'm so happy for you two. You know we love Kate," Mom says. "How do you feel?"

"I'd love nothing more. If she does accept, I'm thinking about proposing to her."

"Fantastic!" my dad shouts. "Congratulations!"

My mom claps her hands and covers her mouth, and I swear I see her eyes tear up. "When are you going to ask her?"

"She hasn't accepted the job yet." I laugh. "I want her to be sure about the life change. But if she does, I'm sure I'll know when the time is right."

"Oh, Justin! This is so exciting! We didn't know if you and Kate would ever get married. She is such a wonderful woman!" Mom exclaims.

"I'm glad you both approve."

"There's nothing that would make us happier. Except maybe a few grandchildren," Dad jokes.

"Let's don't be rushing things, Dad." I smile. "One step at a time."

"You'll call us the minute you know something?" Mom asks.

"Yes, I will."

"What's the case you're working on?" Dad asks. "You said you had some questions for your mother."

"There's a man in his late thirties who's been arrested for multiple murders. What's interesting is that he has no background information that can be verified. It's as if he never existed. Every time I get another lead into his identity, I come up empty. I really believe he's taken on another person's identity. I also think he's not really hiding or covering up. It's like he's become this other person. I was hoping Mom could enlighten me a little."

"I'm sure she can. I'll have to turn this over to Dr. Sigmund Freud," Dad jokes. "Please take over, Doctor."

"Well, I was wondering," I say. "How common is it for someone to take on another's identity, and can this type of person be dangerous?"

"There's a personality disorder called imposter syndrome," Mom says. "It's a psychological pattern when someone hates his life and is convinced he's a fraud. A lot of times, it comes from a bad childhood or a broken home. It could also be related to drug or alcohol abuse. People with an antisocial personality may exhibit these tendencies. They feel guilty and undeserving, so they assume another's identity. With this disorder, it's not unusual for them to make up stories about their life to feel better about themselves. You can see examples of this in a person's workplace. Someone might act out another lifestyle at work that can be quite different from reality. As with every disorder, there are many degrees. One person might just put on a different personality in certain situations due to low self-esteem. Another might take it further.

"This happened in the true case of Ferdinand Waldo Demara Jr., played by Tony Curtis in the movie *The Great Imposter*. Demara had many different identities. After quitting high school, he joined the army with fake papers. Once detected, he stole the identity of a monk, a sailor, a prison warden, a teacher, and a doctor. He claimed he did it for the adventure."

"Can someone with this type of disorder actually commit murder?" I ask.

"Personality disorders are quite common. The problem arises with the overlap of other mental disorders."

"Like someone being paranoid?" I ask.

"Exactly. People with schizophrenia might hear voices or noises and become paranoid. They might think they have unusual powers or that others control their thoughts. It's a breakdown between thought, emotion, and behavior. This leads them to a faulty perception of reality. The result can be hallucinations and delusions.

"There are four types of schizophrenia, all in varying degrees. Paranoid schizophrenia would be more in line with criminal tendencies. A person's paranoia may be extreme, and he might act on it."

"Something like an angel of death?" my dad asks.

"That is an example," Mom answers. "People often cite voices telling them that through their act of mercy, the patient will no longer suffer and will be free of the pains of the evil world. They justify their actions by bending reality into their own perceptions. What is perceived is true."

"How is it diagnosed?" my dad asks.

"It has to be diagnosed by a psychiatrist. Usually one with a specialty in this area. Even then, it's not an easy process. It can take multiple sessions just to identify the type of schizophrenia. From there, the professional must break down the degree of severity and some possible causes and must also determine if this individual is dangerous to himself or someone else."

"Can these people be treated successfully?" I ask.

"As in the case of paranoid schizophrenia, most people need lifelong treatment with antipsychotic drugs, counseling, and social rehabilitation. Others require commitment to mental hospitals or hospitals for the criminally insane. About one-third of people with schizophrenia don't believe anything is wrong with them and never seek help."

"Thanks, Mom. That gives me a lot to think about. I might call you if something in my investigation seems strange or out of place."

"How is your job going?" my dad asks. "You mentioned on the phone you're having an issue with Rocco again. What's going on?"

"Rocco is being Rocco. He's just so overbearing. Lately, he's been changing my articles. Sometimes the changes don't represent the truth. Not like he's publishing false information, but he presents them awfully close to the edge. He leaves out facts and leads the reader to draw a different conclusion. He says he's just giving the readers what they want. It's all about selling papers, not presenting the whole truth. It's been bothering me more lately."

"Do you think it bothers you because your name is attached to the article?"

"Yes, I'm sure of that. I spend a lot of time investigating and researching information before I send an article to him. And it's like with a swipe of the pen, the article isn't mine anymore."

"Yet you're listed as the author."

"Exactly."

I hear the phone ring inside, and Mom gets up from her seat. "You two can talk about this without me. I'm sure you'll do the right thing. Don't leave without saying goodbye."

"Okay, Mom."

"Well," my dad says, "you do work for a tabloid. Please don't take this wrong, but they're not known for always presenting all the information. I've been enormously proud of your work. You've done a fantastic job. If you're not happy with what you're doing, my advice would be to look for another alternative."

"I know. That's the conclusion I keep coming up with. But I just don't know where to start. I love what I do."

"If you love what you do, then the question becomes who do you want to do it for? Who has the biggest newspaper circulation in the area?"

"I'd have to say the *Times-Picayune*."

"You can be assured they know your name from your work at the *Chronicle*. Maybe you could put out a few feelers. I bet they would love to have an investigative reporter with your talent."

"Thanks, Dad. I need to put all my time and effort into the case I'm on now, but once I finish, I believe I will."

Giving my dad a hug, I get ready for my trip back to NOLA. "Love you, Dad. I'll go see Mom before I leave."

"Love you too, Son. Don't stay away so long. Maybe we can get a game of golf in on your next trip."

"I'll set some time aside."

"We're excited about you and Kate. Let us know as soon as something happens."

"I will. I'm excited too."

After saying goodbye to my mom, I head toward the Webster Apartments in New Orleans. Along the way, I keep thinking about the *Times-Picayune*. I know a reporter who works there. I could meet him for lunch one day and get some inside information on the paper. It would make sense for me to start with the *Times-Picayune*. I've always admired their articles. From what I've read, they do thorough research and report the facts. They also have a section on social issues, which requires investigative reporting. It's along the lines of what I'm currently doing but includes a search for social justice. If, through my investigation, I can influence an issue in a way that leads to reform, that will give me a feeling of accomplishment. That type of reporting interests me, but I know I should put it on the back burner. Right now, I must keep my mind focused on Morone. There's still a lot to discover.

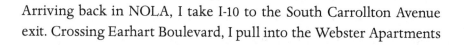

Arriving back in NOLA, I take I-10 to the South Carrollton Avenue exit. Crossing Earhart Boulevard, I pull into the Webster Apartments

parking lot. Checking the information from Teresa McCall's vehicle registration, I locate her old apartment in building C. She was in one of two downstairs apartments. I knock on the door of the apartment across from hers, and an elderly man greets me. I explain who I am and say I'm following up on the recent death of Ms. McCall. As we exchange names, his wife appears.

"We were so sorry to hear about Teresa. She was a beautiful woman," his wife says.

"So you knew her?" I ask.

"Oh yes. She would help me with my groceries sometimes. She was so thoughtful and nice. She would bring us cookies over when she was baking. It was just horrible what happened."

"Did you ever see her with someone? A boyfriend perhaps?"

"No, but we did meet one of her friends from work. A foreign woman. Looked Asian but spoke perfect English."

"Do you remember her name?"

"Yes, her name was Danielle. Teresa called her Dee."

"Do you remember anything else about Teresa or Dee that may be helpful?"

"No, I don't think so. What about you, Franklin?" she asks her husband.

"No, I never saw her with anybody but Dee," he replies.

"Did the police ever question you about Teresa?"

"No, we weren't here when it happened. We were visiting my sister in Tennessee. We found out about it when we got home. I hope they find whoever did this. We've been staying in at night. It's just frightening."

"Thank you both for talking with me." I hand them one of my cards. "If you remember anything else, please call me."

"We will," she responds.

After leaving the apartment complex, I head over to the minimarket by the airport, hoping to catch up with Dee. Dominic never mentioned her in our conversation. Maybe this is the evidence he keeps referring to.

When I arrive, it's midafternoon. Entering the store, I see three employees. An Asian woman is restocking the counter by the coffee makers. As I approach, I see her name tag: Dee. I interrupt her work and explain who I am and why I'm here. I extend my sympathies for the loss of her friend and ask if she can find the time to speak with me. As I hand her my business card, she tells me she's getting off in twenty minutes and will speak with me outside at the picnic table. After thanking her for her time, I buy a bag of chips and a cold drink. Taking a seat outside, I munch on my snacks and wait.

Twenty minutes later, she exits the market and takes a seat across from me. I emphasize again how sorry I am for her loss.

"Thank you. It was quite a shock when I read it in the papers. I couldn't believe what I was reading. I remember calling the newspaper to confirm they had the right name. You hear about things like this happening, but you never think it could happen to someone you know."

"Yes, I understand what you mean. I had a close friend who served with me in the army. He was killed in a shooting when he was back home. As a soldier, I can accept the fact of someone being killed on the battlefield—not that it's easy, but you realize there'll be casualties. It was much harder for me to rationalize that we came home, and my friend lost his life in a senseless shooting."

"That's sad. I'm sorry." She looks off into the distance for a minute and then returns her gaze to me. "How can I help? I don't think there's any more I can add that I haven't already told the police."

"I spoke with Detective Dominic DeAngelis earlier, and I just wanted to verify several things. Do you remember Detective DeAngelis?"

"Yes, he was genuinely nice. He took my statement and asked questions about Teresa. He seemed confident that they would find her murderer and that the courts would put him away for good."

"How did you meet Teresa?"

"She interviewed for a position here at the market when she moved to New Orleans from Meridian. I trained her on second shift, and we became friends."

"Do you remember when that was?"

"It was around the middle of December. Before Christmas. I can look up the date if you need me to."

"No, that's not necessary. I'm sure I can find it in the report. I spoke with an elderly couple who lived across from her at the Webster Apartments. Do you remember them?"

"Oh yes." She smiles. "Margie and Franklin. They're a nice couple. Teresa would bake cookies and always took some over to them. They loved the attention."

"Did Teresa date anyone or have a boyfriend?"

"She had a few dates but not anything like a boyfriend. She wasn't seeing anyone on a regular basis."

"According to the police report, she had a recent tattoo of a crescent moon. Do you know where she got that tattoo?"

"Yes, we had a day off and went to the French Quarter. Teresa had never been there. There was a shop named Carnal Ink, and we stopped in. Next thing I know, she's getting a tattoo." She laughs. "Teresa was like that. She was very spontaneous. That's what I really loved about her. She was unpredictable."

"Do you remember the name of the tattoo artist or what he looked like?"

"Yes, his name was Andre. Short hair and a goatee. Had a scar over his eye. Very strange if you ask me."

"Could he have been one of her dates?"

"Yes, they got to talking, and she told him she was new to New Orleans and the area. He offered to show her the French Quarter and some of the great entertainment bars. She said she would like that and gave him her number."

"Did you both go out with him?"

"No, he called her a few days later, and they set a date."

"Do you remember when they went out?"

"It was in early January. I remember because there was a concert we were talking about going to, but we weren't able to get tickets."

"Do you know how many times they may have been out together?"

"Yes, they went out twice. Teresa said he was too weird for her."

"How so?"

"Don't know. She just said he was weird and wouldn't go out with him anymore."

"Do you remember when the second time was that they went out?"

"It was around Valentine's Day in February. A lot of the bars were having Valentine's parties. That was the last time she saw him."

"Do you know if he continued to call her?"

"She said he called her a few days later, but she told him she wasn't interested."

"Did he contact her after that?"

"She never mentioned that he did. She broke it off, and that was that."

"Did he ever come by the market?"

"I never saw him here."

"Do you know if he picked her up at her apartment the night they went out?"

"She said she was going to meet him in the Quarter."

"Did she mention where they were going to meet?"

"No, she didn't mention where."

"And you told all this to Detective DeAngelis?"

"Yes, the second time."

"So he interviewed you more than once?"

"Yes, the first time was shortly after the incident. He interviewed everyone who worked here. The last time was several days ago. He wanted to know more about her friends and if I knew where she had gotten her last tattoo. He said there was some new evidence that he was following up on. I saw in the paper that they had arrested someone. Do you think Andre may be involved?"

"The police are looking for him for questioning. That's all I know."

"I hope they find him. Is there anything else I can help you with? I'd like to get home."

"No, you have been extremely helpful. I know it's hard for you to talk about, but I appreciate your time. If you remember anything else or see Andre, please call me."

"I will."

After Dee leaves, I mull over the information. If Andre was out with Teresa, it's easy to conclude he may have followed her home and found out where she lived. I don't think she would have told him her address, since she met him in the Quarter. At that point, she was still unsure about him. If she broke off their relationship early on, as Dee mentioned, the only logical conclusion is that he followed her home, probably without her knowing.

I'm amused when I think about Dominic going back for a second interview after I gave him the information on Andre LeBlanc and the common tattoo found on each victim. He followed up. It probably hurt his ego that he missed an important suspect in the investigation. I can understand why he never revealed this to me. Admission will hide behind pride.

I start to call him but know better. *Don't poke the sleeping bear.*

I finish my snacks and get a call as I leave the market. "The bear is awake." I laugh.

"Hi, Detective. What's up?"

"I've been meeting with Jeff, the narc agent, all day. Early this morning, he conducted a major bust on our friend Viper. I wanted to fill you in."

"Do I need to come by your office?"

"No, I'm tied up for several more hours, but I can cover most of it over the phone. I can send you a copy of the transcripts later when they become available. Can you talk now?"

"Absolutely. Go ahead."

"As you know, Jeff was working undercover. Viper was dealing in some small stuff but had contacted a couple of druggies dealing in meth and cocaine. Jeff and his group busted one of the dealers early this morning after Viper made a buy. We rounded up Viper's goth buddies for questioning. There'll be additional indictments issued for their involvement. There were also stolen goods, cash, and guns confiscated that involved the bartender at the Cave, Matthew Sims. Sims was the fence. He's also in custody."

"This is great news. I'm glad Viper is off the street. Did you find out anything related to the Morone case?"

"No, but I picked up Andre LeBlanc's cousin Willy for questioning. I wanted to get to him before he finds out about Viper and splits.

Information runs fast in small groups. I'm letting him sit right now and stew awhile. I'll let you know if I find out any more.

"One more thing: Morone's attorney is having psychiatric testing done on him. I'm sure he's setting up his defense on insanity. He doesn't have any other options. I'm going to push Willy hard. I need to locate LeBlanc to put this case to bed."

"LeBlanc is certainly a major part of this. If I find out anything, I'll call you immediately."

After hanging up with Dominic, I head home to have some dinner, work on my article, and wait for a call from Kate. I have a meeting with Morone in a few days, but I want to have the interview with Bill Tamboli's mother first. Without her input, I don't have a lot of new questions for Morone.

It is almost nine o'clock that night when Kate phones. She's excited and wants to know if I can meet her at her house. After saving the information I'm working on, I hit the door running.

When I arrive, Kate is on her front porch, talking on her phone. As I approach, I hear her tell her mom bye. Jumping into my arms, she gives me a passionate kiss. I notice a tear in her eye.

"I hope those are happy tears."

"They are!" She laughs. "Come inside, and I'll tell you all about it."

"It must have been a good dinner."

"It was perfect! My interview went great, and the board wants to meet with me again before making an official offer."

"That's moving fast."

"The director said they would like to make an offer before the semester ends, so I can work with the current dean before he leaves. She said the job is mine if I want it."

"Did you talk about your photography business and your website?"

"Yes, she loved the idea of having students able to work in real-life situations. She asked me to put together a student involvement curriculum that can be presented to the president and the board of trustees. She said she will do her part in helping to ensure the program is approved."

"With your contacts, it will be a great opening for graduates to work an internship while they're pursuing an advanced education. It sounds like a win-win situation. I think the board will see it that way too."

"I'm sorry—would you like something to drink? I'm getting a glass of red wine."

"A half glass would be great."

I can tell Kate has deliberated on the outcome of her decision and is ready for a life change. My thoughts turn to us and what the future holds. When Kate returns with the wine, we sit in silence for a while. My question burns inside me.

"Where do you see us in the future?" I ask.

Kate laughs before answering. "I'm not laughing at your question; it's just that my mom asked me the same question ten minutes ago. My parents love you very much and would like nothing more than to see us make a permanent commitment. I would like that too. I know in the past, I've been the one who wasn't ready. I didn't think it would be fair to you while I was traveling and chasing my career. Running my own business has been stressful. Despite all the positive aspects, there's always that overwhelming pressure of the next paycheck. Where is my next job going to come from, and is it something I want to do or must do? I'm ready when you are."

I feel my face flush as my heart picks up its pace. After all these years, I can clearly see our future. I don't know every aspect of what life holds for us, but whatever it holds, we can work it out together. I still must work out my own situation with Rocco and the *Chronicle*, but for now, it seems unimportant.

"I've been ready since the day we met. I want nothing more than to be with you every day of my life."

Kate smiles and extends her hand out to mine. "Do I hear a proposal in there?"

Taking her hand, I look into her eyes. "Yes, you do. Kate, will you marry me?"

"I will. Forever and always."

Jumping up to kiss her, I bump the table and knock over both glasses of wine; Kate's spills onto her lap. We both laugh as we embrace.

"That will be a proposal to remember." I laugh again.

Kate looks down at her T-shirt and jeans. "I have to get a picture of this. It's proof of our commitment. I just wish I could have gotten one of your face. It was definitely worth a thousand words."

We both laugh again as Kate takes a dozen pictures. She has me pose with every funny face I can make. She even stages the camera and sets up a time-delay photo of me kneeling in front of her, all stained in red wine. I can see this one being the hit of our party.

I clean up my mess as Kate goes to change her clothes and call her mom. Sitting by myself, I have time to reflect. More questions occupy my mind. When are we going to get married? What if she doesn't get the job? Where are we going to live? What about my job? What about the Morone case? I lean back in my chair and smile. "One step at a time," I say out loud. "We'll take it one step at a time."

I pour us another bit of wine and set the glasses on the table. Standing over the back of my chair, I give my parents a call. My dad answers. I can hear the TV in the background.

"I hope it's not too late, but I wanted to tell you that I proposed to Kate, and she accepted."

"Hold on. I'll get your mom so you can tell her."

"Who is it?" I hear my mother ask.

"It's Justin," my dad replies.

"What's he doing calling so late? Is he okay?"

"I'm not sure," my dad jokes. "Says he needs to talk with you."

"Justin, what's happened? Is everything okay?"

"Yes, Mom. Everything is great. Kate and I just got engaged, and I wanted you to know."

"Oh, Justin, I'm so happy for you both! You guys gave me a scare." She laughs. "Have you set a date yet?"

"No, Mom. One step at a time." I laugh.

"I can't tell you how happy we are. Please ask Kate to call me tomorrow. We have so much planning to do."

"Mom, you know Kate's mother will be planning the event with her."

"Oh, I know, but there must be something I can do."

"I'll let you girls work that out. I need to hang up; I hear Kate coming back into the room. I'll call you tomorrow. Love you, Mom."

"I love you too."

When Kate enters the room, I can tell she's been crying. She hugs me again, and I hear a whimper. I squeeze her tightly to reassure her that all is well. "I hope that was a good conversation with your mom," I say.

"Yes, it was extremely good. She was so happy that she started crying. When she started, I started too." She laughs. "She was so excited about the new job and the engagement that she was struggling to keep her composure and handed the phone off to Dad. I'll go by there tomorrow morning. I'm sure she'll be calling me before breakfast. I heard you talking in here. Did you call your parents?"

"Yes, they had the same reaction. I promised to call them tomorrow. Of course, my mother wants you to call her too. I said you would."

"I was going to. I'm sure we're all going to have dinner soon."

"Oh yeah. That goes without saying."

Kate sits back down.

I raise my wineglass. "To us. If our life is only half of my dreams, it will be fantastic."

Kate smiles and raises her glass in a toast.

"Do we need to talk about a date?" I ask.

"I told my mother I would like to get settled into my new job first, if that's okay with you."

"I'm good with that. I just wanted to be sure we're both on the same page when we talk with our friends and family."

"I did talk with my mom about having a church wedding. I really would like to have one. Are you okay with that?"

"I'm very much okay with that. I've been thinking a lot lately about going to see Father Vic at Our Lady of the Rosary. I understand he's still there. Do you remember him?"

"Father Vic will be great. I know that will please our parents. Church is a part of my life I've missed. Thank you."

"I'd better be going. I know you have a lot to think about and have to start work on a presentation for a curriculum. Maybe Saturday we can look at rings and have lunch at City Park. I've always loved spending time with you there. It's always been relaxing to me."

"That sounds great. It's a date."

After a little more discussion about her job offer, I finish my wine and head home. I'm hoping to meet up with Dominic tomorrow to go over the transcripts of the interrogation. I also want to find out more about the drug bust and the relationship between Viper and the Cave's bartender, Matt Sims. Tomorrow will be another busy day. But my dreams tonight will be with Kate.

CHAPTER 10

At seven thirty the next morning, I get a call from Dominic. We agree to meet at his office in an hour to cover his interview with Willy and answer any questions I have about Viper. Although the information on Viper may be interesting, I don't see it progressing the Morone case. Viper's knowledge of LeBlanc and Willy is probably drug-related or through their initial contact at Carnal Ink. As for the Morone case, I believe LeBlanc acted independently of Viper. Willy, on the other hand, has direct knowledge of LeBlanc, and I believe, as Dominic does, he knows LeBlanc's whereabouts.

Upon arriving at the department, I buzz the receptionist and announce my appointment. Within a few minutes, Dominic pushes open the front glass door. After we greet each other, I follow him back into a conference room.

"How about a coffee?" he asks.

"Yes, thanks. I could use one," I reply.

"Break room to your right," he says, gesturing outside the conference room door. "I'll be back in a minute. I need to get my files."

The break room is empty of people. Two pots of coffee sit on an electric burner against the back wall, aligned with a microwave and adjoining sink. Another side counter displays a box of doughnuts, with four pastries remaining, and a smaller box containing three bagels. A Coke machine, a stainless-steel refrigerator, and a candy machine stand at the counter's end. Six tables with chairs fill the rest of the room.

After pouring my coffee, I head back to the conference room as Dominic enters with a handful of file folders. Mumbling something I don't understand, he crushes a couple of empty coffee cups left on the table and throws them into a garbage can by the door.

After a few exchanges of earlier information, Dominic opens a file folder. "Viper's rap is pretty much cut and dried. The narcs have been following him for quite a while. He put his hand into the fire when he started meeting with one of the meth dealers. After that, it was just a matter of time before he burned himself. One of his snake buddies was with him at the time of the buy and will also be indicted. They are looking at a class-B felony with potential prison time of eight to thirty years and a fine of up to a hundred thousand dollars.

"Three more of his snakes will be charged with possession of marijuana. Under federal drug laws, marijuana is classified as a schedule-one drug. A first-possession offense carries misdemeanor penalties of imprisonment for up to one year and a minimum thousand-dollar fine.

"The dealer and two of his clowns will be put away for a long time. They will be indicted for multiple felony charges and distribution of narcotics."

"That should put a dent in the drug population," I say.

"I wish," Dominic replies.

"Do you see any overlap between Viper and Morone?" I ask.

"No, I don't. Viper admits to knowing Andre LeBlanc but not Morone. He still insists it was Morone he saw at the hotel the night of the first murder. With this felony charge over his head, his testimony will be thrown out."

Thinking his testimony is worthless as far as I'm concerned, I opt to keep my mouth shut about Viper and move on. "You mentioned yesterday that the bartender, Matt Sims, had his hand in the pot. Can you tell me a little more about his involvement?"

"Matt Sims was working with a couple of Viper's snakes. We found cash, stolen goods, and guns in a house they were renting and more in a storage shed that was registered to Matt. He confessed to being the fence and selling the stolen goods for a percentage. They had a nice little scam going on. There'll also be an investigation into the owner of the Cave to determine if he had any knowledge or involvement. There were some questionable items found on the property that are being checked out."

"Did Matt have any contact with Morone or LeBlanc?" I ask.

"He claims he doesn't know either of them, and for now, we have no evidence to the contrary."

"That brings us to LeBlanc's cousin Willy. What's your take on him?"

Dominic closes one file folder and opens another. "You may be interested in finding out that Mr. William Montague, a.k.a. Willy, has a nice little rap sheet. Seems he's been involved in several thefts, a couple of misdemeanors, a DUI, and an assault. He claims that he doesn't know Morone but that his cousin LeBlanc mentioned his name to him. When I asked about the conversation, Willy stated that LeBlanc had just said he was helping Morone with a construction job. He didn't know what they were doing or where the job was. He thought it was last January but couldn't remember for sure."

"Since you still don't have LeBlanc in custody, I have to conclude that Willy wasn't open as to his whereabouts," I say.

"Not yet, but we're close. After pulling together all the different phone numbers in Willy's phone records, we have a block of ten square miles on the north end of the city. I believe LeBlanc is within this border. He'll have to come out sooner or later to get supplies or have them delivered. We have street cameras and a surveillance team watching for his next move. We'll get him."

"Do you know if Willy had any contact with the three victims?"

"No, he claims he didn't know any of them and had never been to the market by the airport. We were also able to confirm his alibi on two of the three murder dates. I believe his only involvement with LeBlanc is withholding information. We turned him loose for now, hoping he'll lead us to him. As soon as we find LeBlanc, we'll pick up Willy." Dominic closes the file folder. "Looks like this case will be closed, and you can finish your story." He smiles. "Any questions?"

"I was wondering what information you may have gained from the Carnal Ink DVD video recorder."

"No real information. The previous recordings were recorded over so many times the shadow information was unreadable. It was a dead end."

"Do you think it was recorded over on purpose? Maybe with the intent of hiding something?"

"I don't think so. The DVD was old and showed a lot of handling."

"The more I think about the owner, Jim Carnes, the more I believe he could have had contact with the victims. LeBlanc and Willy both worked for him. I was thinking about going by to talk with him again."

Dominic gives me an odd look, as if considering my statement. "Go for it." He smiles. "Just don't run him out of town." He laughs. "He'll probably be called in as a witness." Shuffling his folders, Dominic gives a sigh of relief. "Anything else?"

"No, it sounds like a clean sweep. I still hope to meet with Bill Tamboli's mother. I believe it will clear up some unanswered questions about Morone's identity."

"Suit yourself, but it won't change the outcome. I'm sure it'll make a good story. You know how to reach me. I have another meeting in a few minutes. Please check out with the receptionist before leaving the building."

Dominic stands up and gathers his folders. He seems confident this case is about to close. I'm still not convinced.

After checking out with the receptionist, I head to the French Quarter. I'm able to find a parking space at the Central Parking System on Conti Street. From there, it's a short walk to Carnal Ink.

The streets are starting to fill with the afternoon crowd. Barkers are giving out discount tickets for merchandise and food. The time between breakfast and lunch has always been my favorite time for people-watching. It's like watching a New York play as the barkers entertain the crowds, some with magic, others with songs, and some with jokes. The bigger the crowd, the louder they bark. Often, there's one hidden inside the place of business. His job is to keep the laughter and noise spilling into the street. The rowdier the bar, the more tourists it attracts. After all, they come to NOLA to let the good times roll.

When I enter Carnal Ink, I'm addressed by one of the artists. "Can I help you?" he asks.

I recognize him from my last visit. "I was checking to see if Jim Carnes was busy. My name is Justin Lancer. I met you last time I was here. If I remember correctly, your name is Nate?"

"Yeah, that's right, but Jim isn't here. He said he was going to settle an account over at Vaping and Tattoos and then catch some lunch. He should be back around one o'clock. You want to leave your card?"

"No, but I was wondering if Jim has a financial interest in Vaping and Tattoos."

"Don't know. All I know is that we help some of the other stores when they need something. We trade back and forth. Mostly ink colors."

"Were you here when Andre's cousin Willy was working here?"

"Yeah, I knew Willy."

"Do you know why he left?"

"No, not really. I think Jim didn't like him for some reason."

"Do you know he's working at Vaping and Tattoos?"

"Yeah, I took some ink by there a couple of weeks ago. I saw him there."

"Does Jim know he works there?"

"Don't know. I never said anything to him about it."

"Thanks, Nate. I'll stop back by after lunch. Maybe I can catch Jim then."

After leaving Carnal Ink, I take a stroll through the Quarter. The smell of food and coffee in the air reminds me that I haven't eaten. I cross over to Royal Street and step inside Café Beignet, where I order a muffuletta on French bread with Genoa salami, ham, Swiss, and provolone, with an olive-salad spread, and add a cup of NOLA's chicory coffee.

As I eat my lunch, my mind races about Jim and Willy. Is there a connection between Jim and the three victims? Was he being truthful with me when he said he fired Willy? Does he have a financial interest in Vaping and Tattoos? Could Jim, LeBlanc, and Willy be running some type of scam? They all know each other. What about the money Jim paid to LeBlanc? Was the payment really for past work, or was it a cover-up or get-out-of-town payment? Jim said he pays his artists in cash when work is done. If that is true, why would he owe LeBlanc back wages?

Finishing my sandwich and coffee, I decide to walk by Vaping and Tattoos and look through the storefront window. Maybe I can spot Jim and Willy and get a better idea of their relationship. I only hope none of Dominic's agents or Willy take notice of me.

When the parlor comes into view, I'm still a good block away. I see Willy standing outside and puffing an e-cigarette. From this vantage point, I can see the front of the store. Not wanting to get closer, I step inside the nearest bar. After ordering a Coke, I take a seat by the window and pretend I'm checking messages on my cell phone. Across the street, I notice a man lingering in front of a clothing store. By his actions, I tag him as an agent. I keep my head down to avoid making eye contact.

Within a few minutes, Jim exits Vaping and Tattoos. He stops and speaks to Willy, placing his hand on Willy's shoulder and laughing. This isn't an action between adversaries but one between associates. They talk for a little while longer, and Jim departs. The street agent takes out his cell phone and makes a call. His contact will be another agent who will pick up surveillance on Jim. Casing the street, I can't identify another agent. Deciding not to pursue Jim currently, I leave the bar and head back to my car.

As I approach the Central Parking System, I get a call from Cindy at the office. She tells me the mayor of Hammond has reached Alice Lane, Bill Tamboli's mother, and she is willing to speak with me.

I immediately work my way to I-55 North toward Hammond. I exit onto Highway 190 East and pick up Wood Scale Road. Alice Lane's house sits on the left of the road, about a mile from Highway 190. The single-story house appears to be an early wood-siding home with a covered front porch. Painted gray concrete steps, set between two circular support columns, are adorned with potted plants. A porch swing and two rocking chairs with a common square table are adjacent to the front window. The white-painted wood siding is immaculate.

After knocking gently on the screen door, I receive acknowledgment in less than a minute. Approaching the screen is a thin golden-haired woman of sixty. She is dressed in an attractive navy-blue pantsuit, with a small string of white pearls around her neck.

"Hello, Mrs. Lane. I'm Justin Lancer."

"Please come in, Mr. Lancer. I'm Alice's sister, Margaret Sales. Alice went to change her clothes. We just got home from shopping."

"Thank you so much for seeing me. I hope I haven't disrupted your shopping day."

"Not at all. We just went into town for lunch at the retirement center, and Alice wanted to drop by the fabric store. She's quite a seamstress."

Margaret leads me into the front room and turns off the TV. "Please have a seat, Mr. Lancer. Would you like a glass of lemon-flavored iced tea or water?"

"Tea would be great. Thank you."

"Make yourself at home. I'll be right back. Alice should be here in a moment."

Taking a seat on a green fabric-covered parlor chair, I pick up a picture from an oak side table. It appears to be an early picture of Alice; her son, Bill; and her sister. More pictures are aligned on the fireplace mantelpiece. The painted plaster walls are mint green. A couch and two more chairs form a semicircle around an oak coffee table that sits upon an oval-shaped throw rug. On the table are several magazines and a family Bible. The decorative floral window curtains drop to the wood floor and appear custom-made. The overhead five-light chandelier illuminates the room, sharpened by two brass floor lamps covered in pale-yellow-fringed lampshades.

As Mrs. Lane enters the room, I stand to show respect and introduce myself. The two sisters could almost be twins.

"Please, Mr. Lancer, have a seat. I don't know what I can do to help, but I'll be glad to contribute whatever information I have."

"I hope you don't mind if I take some notes as we talk. It helps me when I think back on my conversation."

"Not at all, Mr. Lancer. I often have to make notes to myself these days." She laughs.

Alice's sister enters the room and sets a tray with three glasses of tea on the coffee table. After handing me a glass, she sits next to Alice on the couch.

"I think you have met my sister, Margaret. She lives here with me."

"Yes, I have. And I must say, you have a beautiful home."

"Thank you. It was our family home. Margaret and I grew up here and just recently redecorated."

"Your sister told me you're quite a seamstress. Did you make the window curtains? They're magnificent."

"Shame on you, Margaret, for filling this man with nonsense." Alice laughs. "Margaret is the decorator. I made the curtains, and she did all the rest."

"Well, the house is stunning. You certainly complement each other."

"Thank you, Mr. Lancer," Alice replies. "How can I help you?"

"I'm trying to find information on a man by the name of Raymond Morone. He claims he graduated from Picayune High School the same year as your son. Does that name mean anything to you?"

"No, I can't say it does," Alice replies. "How about you, Margaret? Do you remember that name?"

"No, I don't," answers Margaret. "Why do you think we might know him?"

"This Raymond Morone also claims he and Bill were best friends."

"Well, that makes no sense," Alice says. "If he had been my Bill's best friend, we would have known him."

"Did Bill play sports or maybe hang out with some of the kids at school?"

"No, he didn't play sports in high school," Alice says. "If anyone hung out with him, it would have been his cousin Frankie. Those two boys were inseparable. They used to sleep over together when we lived in Picayune. Frankie was broken when Bill was killed. It was Frankie's stepfather who killed my son, Bill, in the car crash. Frankie was never the same after that. He was admitted into a psychiatric hospital and underwent shock treatments for his depression. He had such a sad life."

"What was Frankie's last name?" I ask.

"Benson," Alice replies. "His birth father's name was Thomas Herman Benson. His mother's name was Anna Bridges. Thomas died of lung cancer when Frankie was ten. Anna later married Dwayne Johnson. It was Dwayne who killed my son, Bill. Dwayne was a known drinker, and his autopsy results showed he was drunk at the time of the accident."

"I read the report from the accident. I'm deeply sorry for your loss."

"Thank you."

"How were Bill and Frankie related?" I ask.

"Bill's great-grandfather, our grandfather, and Frankie's great-grandfather was Edwin Michael Sales. Bill and Frankie were second cousins."

"You mentioned that Frankie would stay over sometimes when you lived in Picayune."

"Yes, that's right. He stayed with us the last year of school," Alice replies. "Tension was pretty bad between Frankie and his mom and stepdad."

"I hope you don't mind, but I drove by the property in Picayune and by Bill's grave site. May I ask you a question about the headstone?"

"No, I don't mind."

I pull up the picture on my phone that shows the damage cut into the stone. "I was wondering if you've seen the X cut into the headstone. It appears to have been done with a shape tool. Probably a chisel."

Both Alice and Margaret examine the photo, passing the phone back and forth a few times.

"Yes, I saw it for the first time around Christmas of last year," Alice responds. "I told Margaret about it, but this is the first time she's seen it."

"I also found a similar mark on the water pump door at the property in Picayune," I say, pulling up that photo. I show it to the sisters.

"I remember this one." Margaret speaks up. "I was helping at the house in Picayune, when I discovered blood in the bathroom sink. I called Bill's dad, John, and told him that something terrible had happened. John rushed home and went searching for the boys. He showed me the drops of blood on the pump house door and the X. When he found the boys playing by the pond, he found out they had cut their thumbs with a pocketknife to become blood brothers."

Alice gets a strange look on her face. "Do you think Frankie was the one who cut the X into Bill's headstone?"

"Yes, I do," I say. "Do you have any pictures of Frankie around the house?"

"No, I don't think so," Alice replies. She turns to Margaret. "Do you know of any?"

"Heavens no. We didn't know Frankie was still alive. After he was released from the hospital, he stayed with his grandparents for about a week and then left. They found a note on the table telling them he was leaving. He stole money from the house, some of Lester's astronomy books, and his telescope. We never heard or saw him again. It was terrible what that boy went through."

"You lost me," I reply. "Who is Lester?"

"I'm sorry," Margaret says. "Bill's grandfather Albert Benson had his sister, Beth, and brother-in-law, Lester, living with him. The boys loved Lester. He was a retired science teacher, and the boys often spent hours with him, looking through his telescope from the hayloft at night. Lester was a wonderful teacher, and the boys learned a lot about the night sky and star constellations."

"I always thought those two would end up as astronomers," Alice says. "Ray was a big influence on their life."

"What a minute. Who is Ray?" I ask.

The sisters laugh.

"I guess we have you very confused by now." Alice smiles. "Albert's brother-in-law was Lester Raymond Miron. We all called him Ray."

"Is Lester still living?" I ask.

"No, he died in an unfortunate accident. He was in the barn and somehow tripped in the hayloft and fell to the barn floor. A sickle was found in his neck. Frankie was the one who found him. All Frankie's ancestors have died. We're not sure about his mother. She left before Frankie got out of the hospital. Frankie lived such a tragic life. Three deaths in less than a year. He just couldn't handle it."

"Do you know Frankie's mother's maiden name, by any chance?"

"I believe it was Shepard," Alice says. "Yes, it was Anna Marie Shepard."

"Is the farmhouse where Frankie's grandparents and family lived still here in Hammond?" I ask.

"No, the barn burned down a long time ago. The house was torn down, and a co-op tractor supply was built on the site," Alice answers.

"There seem to be a lot of fires around here. Between the house in Picayune, the high school, and the barn," I say.

"Yes, that is odd," Margaret agrees.

"Can you tell me if Frankie's grandparents and family are buried in Hammond?"

"Yes, they are. They're buried at Valley Grove Cemetery, just outside Hammond. Not far from here. Why do you ask?" Alice says.

"Sometimes it's easier to verify names and dates by checking information on headstones. Most of the time, you can be assured the information is correct. Miron is a strange name. Do you know where that name originates?"

"Ray claimed he was Italian, but it sounds more French to me," Margaret answers.

"Mrs. Lane, did Bill date a girl with the initials DC? There was a heart carved into the pump house door with BT + DC inside. Do you know who DC might be?"

Alice turns to Margaret. "The girl Bill went to the prom with—wasn't her name Donna?"

"Yes, I believe it was," Margaret replies. "But I don't remember her last name."

"It was Creek," Alice says. "It was Donna Creek."

"You wouldn't happen to have a prom picture, would you?" I ask.

"There was one in the yearbook," Margaret answers.

"Yes, that's right," Alice says.

"You have a copy of Bill's senior yearbook?" I ask.

"Yes," Alice replies. "I believe it's in a box in the hall closet." She turns to her sister for confirmation, and Margaret nods in agreement.

"That would mean Frankie's picture will also be in there. May I please see the yearbook?"

"Of course," replies Alice. "Margaret, be a doll and get the box down from the top shelf."

"I want to thank you, Mrs. Lane. You and your sister have been a tremendous help to me."

"You're very welcome," Alice replies. Once Margaret is out of the room, Alice turns to me. "Mr. Lancer, may I ask your opinion about something?"

"Of course, Mrs. Lane."

"Do you think Frankie is back in the area?"

In my mind, I now believe Raymond Morone is Frankie Benson. I also believe that bringing up the information that Frankie is being held on multiple murder charges will serve no purpose. "Yes, Mrs. Lane, I do think he's back in the area. Does his presence concern you?"

"I'm not sure. I feel apprehensive about seeing him again after all these years. The possibility frightens me."

Margaret reenters the room with a green file box. She removes the top and pulls out the 1999 Picayune High School yearbook. After laying it on the coffee table, she pages through the senior pictures. "Here's a picture of Bill. He was a handsome young man, just like his dad."

Below the picture is an ink-written X with the note "Blood brothers for life. FB."

"Look here, Alice," Margaret says. "There's that same *X*."

"Yes, I see it," Alice replies.

Margaret pages back to find Frankie Benson. "Here's a picture of Frankie."

I'm not surprised when I look at the picture of Frankie, who is now Raymond Morone. Even with the passing of nineteen years, there's no question in the resemblance. They're one and the same.

Flipping forward a few pages, Margaret points out Donna Creek. "Here's Donna. Beautiful young lady, isn't she?"

"Yes, she's extremely attractive. Do you know if she or her family still live in the area?"

"No, I don't. Do you, Alice?" Margaret asks her sister.

"No, but I remember she received a scholarship to the University of Tennessee in Knoxville. I believe the family moved there the summer after graduation."

Turning to the front of the book, Margaret finds Bill and Donna's prom picture. "Here are Bill and Donna the night of the prom. They were a beautiful couple."

Bill and Donna are standing under a flower-covered arch. Bill is dressed in a light blue tuxedo with a light blue bow tie. Donna is dressed in a light-blue-and-white prom gown. Her long blonde hair is pulled over to one shoulder. A blue-and-white corsage is laced around her wrist.

"Did Frankie attend the prom?" I ask.

"Yes, he did," Alice answers. "But I don't remember who he was with. Do you, Margaret?"

"No, I don't," Margaret replies. "There's no prom picture of him in the yearbook."

"Ladies, I can't thank you enough for all your help. You've been extremely helpful."

"You're welcome, Mr. Lancer," Alice says. "Is there anything else we can help you with?"

"You mentioned that Lester Raymond Miron is buried in Valley Grove Cemetery. Would you have the plot number, by any chance?"

"I'm sure it's here in the Bible," Alice says. Upon opening the family

Bible, she finds the information. "Yes, here it is. Lester Raymond Miron. Born May 1, 1924, in Tangipahoa Parish, Hammond, Louisiana. Died July 2, 1999, in Tangipahoa Parish, Hammond, Louisiana. Valley Grove Cemetery, Hammond, Louisiana. Plot G23."

Gathering my notes together, I thank the sisters again for their time and leave my card on the table. As I leave the house, I feel an overwhelming sense of accomplishment and satisfaction.

After I take a few more steps, the darkness of the investigation sends a chill through my soul. I feel as if I'm tangled in a spiderweb, waiting for the fangs of venom. An image of Lester on the barn floor with a sickle in his neck is impressed on my mind. A sickle—an object in the shape of a crescent moon. The astronomy books and telescope with the initials *RM* that I saw in Morone's apartment all make sense. What's still unknown is Andre LeBlanc's involvement in all this. Could LeBlanc be setting up Morone for the fall? And how are Jim at Carnal Ink and Willy involved?

Trying to clear my mind, I pull out my cell phone and get directions to Valley Grove Cemetery on my GPS.

Just a few miles outside Hammond, I pull through the iron gates. A map board is just inside. Checking the plots, I locate G23, and then I circle the right side of the cemetery and stop at the seventh section by the back road. Approaching plot G23, I pass several headstones with the surname Benson. Next to Albert Benson, Frankie's grandfather, is the headstone of Lester Raymond Miron. The dates agree with the information I obtained from Mrs. Lane. Above Lester's name are three stars and a crescent moon. As I stare at the symbols, I recall the dream of John the Baptist in which the crescent moon settled on a headstone. His dream was no coincidence.

I google the surname Miron to find its origin. Its origin is European, and it is found in French, Italian, and Spanish Castilian countries. Next, I google the surname Morone. As I stare at the results, I can't believe my eyes. Its origin is Italian, but variations of spelling include the following: Moron, Moro, Morol, Moriles, Morona, Miron, Moroldi, Moroni, Moronati, Morrone, Morroni, and many more.

Frankie has turned the name Lester Raymond Miron into Raymond Lester Morone.

As I arrive back in NOLA, my next move is to follow up with Jim Carnes at Carnal Ink. Dominic didn't tell me to stay away or say Jim is under surveillance.

The evening crowd in the Quarter have already filled the streets. After again parking in the Central Parking System, I head to Carnal Ink. When I arrive, Jim is behind the front counter.

"Hi, Jim. Justin Lancer. I spoke with you before about Andre LeBlanc."

"Sure, I remember. You back for that tattoo? I'll give you a good deal today. How does twenty percent off sound?"

"No, not today."

"If you're here again about Andre, I haven't seen him since he came by and got his back pay. I told that detective, and he said he would tell you. That's all I know."

"Yes, Detective DeAngelis did tell me. I'm here about his cousin Willy. You said he used to work here. Do you know where I can find him?"

"Yes, I ran into him today. He's working at Vaping and Tattoos. I was surprised to find him there."

"That must have been a bigger surprise to him. If I remember, you told me you two had some issues when he left."

"Yeah, but we're all right. He told me he was sorry he left the way he did and asked me not to tell his boss. He seemed sincere and was worried I might get him fired. I agreed not to get involved in his work. He seemed relieved. He even offered to help me out one Saturday for free to set things straight."

"Well, that's great news. I hope it all works out."

"Yeah, I think it will. I'm still glad he works for them and not me. He's not a very dependable employee."

"I also wanted to ask you about Andre."

"Told you all I know. There's no more."

"I was wondering about the back pay he came by to get."

"Not much to it. I owed him some money, and he came by to get it. Case closed."

"It was my understanding that you paid the artists at the end of each day. How is it that you owed him back wages?"

"Hell, I don't pay them every day. Nobody would show up." He laughs. "I pay them twice a week. That keeps them coming back." Jim looks around at some customers coming in the door and excuses himself. "Well, I need to make some money today. Can't make a living by talking." He smiles. "Stop by when you're ready for that tattoo. Offer stands."

"Thanks, Jim. I'll do that."

Once I retrieve my car, I head home to run some background information on Donna Creek. If I can find her, she might be able to tell me who Frankie Benson's prom date was. Hopefully, one of the two can tell me who Frankie Benson was before he was Raymond Morone.

Upon arriving at home, I boot up my computer and run my ancestry program. I'm able to locate Donna's parents' address in Picayune in 1999. In 2000, they moved to Knoxville, Tennessee. She graduated from UT Knoxville in 2005. Doing a deeper search on Donna, I find a recent house purchase, with her address in Maryville, and her phone number. I give her a call. I get her answering machine. It takes me two messages to explain who I am and the purpose of my call. I leave my cell number and hope for a call back.

After thirty minutes, I get my call. At first, Donna is reluctant to speak to me about Bill Tamboli, but once I explain that I met with Bill's mother in Hammond and that she was the one who gave me Donna's name, Donna becomes more receptive.

"How is Mrs. Tamboli?" she asks.

"She is doing fine. She and her sister, Margaret, are living together.

Mrs. Tamboli remarried, and her name is now Lane. She was able to purchase the family home, and she and her sister restored it," I reply.

"She was so nice to me. I was devastated when Bill was killed."

"The whole town shares your feelings. I spoke with Mr. Bo Watkins and his wife, who live on Route 43 in Picayune. They both remembered the night of the accident. You may remember Bo. He ran the general store in Picayune."

"Yes, I remember him. Always had his dog in the store." She laughs.

"One of the reasons I'm calling is to find out about Frankie Benson. Do you remember him?"

"Yes, he and Bill were best friends. We double-dated at the senior prom."

"What can you tell me about Frankie?"

"Not a lot. He was different from most. Some days, he was quiet and didn't speak to you. Other days, he was funny and outgoing. Bill told me he had a tough life and didn't get along with his stepfather. That's about all I remember. He was mostly quiet."

"Do you remember who he went to the prom with?"

"The girl's name was Mary Cotton. She transferred in her senior year from St. Louis. Seems like she worked in Memphis after graduation. She was wanting to pursue something in the medical field."

The name hits me in the gut. Mary Sadler Cotton was the name of the second victim. The information fits the profile I found on her. "Do you know where she worked in Memphis?"

"I believe she was helping out at a psychiatric hospital there while she worked on her degree. I'm not sure which one. Sorry I can't be more help."

"You've been extremely helpful. Thank you so much for your time."

"You're welcome."

As soon as I hang up, I call Mrs. Lane in Hammond. She answers on the third ring.

"Hi, Mrs. Lane. Justin Lancer. I'm sorry to bother you again, but do you remember which hospital Frankie was sent to after his breakdown?"

"Yes, it was the Memphis Psychiatric Hospital. That was where he received those horrible shock treatments. I felt so sorry for him."

"Thank you, Mrs. Lane. I was just confirming some new information."

"You're welcome, Mr. Lancer. Please feel free to call if I can help."

While I'm talking, I get an incoming call from Dominic. After I hang up with Mrs. Lane, I call him back.

"What's up?" I ask.

"We picked up LeBlanc and Willy a few minutes ago. I'm letting LeBlanc sit for an hour before questioning him. We have read him his rights, and he's agreed to talk without representation. He's scared and wanting protection. If you want to observe, be here in thirty minutes."

"I'll be there."

CHAPTER 11

When I arrive at the station, I find that Detective DeAngelis has left information with the receptionist. I receive a pass card and am directed to one of the control booths used for recording the interrogations of suspects. Upon my entering the room, an officer checks my pass card and has me sign in. The room consists of a control desk and four chairs. The walls and ceiling are painted black, with recessed, diffused overhead lighting. I am asked to turn off my cell phone and any sound-emitting devices I have with me. The officer takes his seat at a control desk, puts on a set of headphones, and instructs me to do the same. The headsets are plugged into the control desk, which faces a one-way glass window. From my seat, I have a clear view of the interrogation room.

Within minutes, LeBlanc is brought into the interrogation room by one of the deputies. His wrist shackles are locked onto a half-circle steel rod attached to the table. LeBlanc looks around nervously and twitches in his seat. The deputy stands by the door until Detective DeAngelis enters the room. Dominic places a file of papers on the table and remains standing in silence. LeBlanc keeps his head turned downward and makes no eye contact. After another minute, Dominic takes a seat and opens the file folder.

Dominic begins. "This session is being recorded. You've already been read your rights and have decided to speak with me without counsel. Is that correct?"

"Yes," LeBlanc says.

"Do you understand your rights as they were read to you?"

"Yes."

"Please state your full name."

"Andre Demonte LeBlanc."

"Do you know of a man by the name of Raymond Morone?"

"Yeah."

"How did you come to know him?"

"I met him at a bar. He struck up a conversation, and we talked awhile."

"When was this?"

"It was in November."

"That would be November of 2017?"

"Yes."

"What did you talk about?"

"I was drawing some stuff on a napkin. He seemed interested in it. I told him I was a tattoo artist. He wanted to come by the shop to see some of my images."

"And did he?"

"Yeah, he came by one day. He wanted a tattoo of a two-faced wolf. I made a sketch, and he liked it."

"Did you meet with him again after that?"

"Yeah, we met several times after that. Sometimes for a drink. Sometimes for me to help him with a job."

"What kind of work did you help him with?"

"He had some construction jobs that sometimes required two people. I would help him when I had the time."

"What about welding jobs? Did you ever help him with that kind of work?"

"Yeah, sometimes."

"When was the last welding job you helped him with?"

"I think it was around Christmas. I helped him with a gate."

"Did he ever loan you his truck?"

"Yeah, a couple of times."

"What about his apartment? Did you ever go to his apartment?"

"Yeah."

"Did you ever have a woman with you in the truck or in his apartment?"

LeBlanc's body language changes dramatically. He turns his body to one side and stares off into space. Twenty seconds pass before his outburst. "I didn't kill that girl! Morone is setting me up! I didn't do it!"

Dominic remains quiet for a full thirty seconds. He gives LeBlanc time to recover from his outburst before continuing. "What's the girl's name?"

"Liz!"

"Are you referring to Elizabeth Mary DeBoy?" Dominic slides a picture in front of LeBlanc.

"Yes! That's her. I didn't kill her!"

"I never mentioned that Miss DeBoy was killed. When did you find out she was dead?"

"Just this month."

"And how did you come by this information?"

"When I went by to pick up the money that was owed me. My boss showed me an article in the paper. He asked me if she was the same girl who had been by the shop."

"You're referring to your boss at Carnal Ink, Jim Carnes?"

"Yeah."

"How did you meet Miss DeBoy?"

"Morone introduced her to me at a bar one night. Said she wanted a tattoo. That's all, man! We went out a few times, but I didn't kill her! I swear!"

"Do you know where you were the night of December 31?"

"I was partying like everybody else on New Year's Eve."

"Did you see Morone or Miss DeBoy that night?"

"Yes, I saw them at a bar."

"They were together?"

"Yes."

"Do you know how Miss DeBoy was killed?"

"The article said she was strangled."

"That's correct. What the article didn't say was that she was strangled with nylon rope. The same rope that was found in your possession from the Beesly Hardware robbery."

"That wasn't my rope! I traded for it! It's not my rope!"

"How many rolls of rope did you trade for?"

"It was two or three!"

"Which was it? Two or three?"

"It was three! I got three rolls of rope and some welding stuff!"

"That's an odd trade for a tattoo artist. Why did you trade for welding materials and rope?"

"I thought I could sell it to Morone."

"And did you sell it to Morone?"

"He bought a few things but not all of it."

"Did he buy a roll of rope?"

"Yes, a roll of rope and a couple of tools."

"So let me get this straight. You had three rolls of rope and sold one of them to Morone, along with some tools? Is that what you are saying?"

"Yes."

"When did you come into possession of the items from the Beesly Hardware robbery?"

"I don't know, man! It was either November or December."

"Was it before Christmas?"

"Yes. But it wasn't me! I think Morone killed her!"

"What brings you to that conclusion?"

"He's crazy!"

"His being crazy doesn't mean he killed her. Did you speak to Morone about her death?"

"Yeah. I brought it up, and he said something about her stalking him."

"What did he mean by that?"

"I don't know. I told you: he's crazy. He just stared at me in a strange way and laughed. That was it for me. I never wanted to see him again. I split."

"Did he contact you after that?"

"He called me at work and wanted to meet one night. I told him I was busy. That was when I left Carnal Ink and changed my phone."

"Did you think he was going to harm you?"

"I don't know, but I wasn't going to give him the chance."

"Do you believe he's still looking for you?"

"Yeah."

"Do you know where Morone kept his equipment and supplies?"

"Yeah. He has a storage building on Airline Boulevard. E-Z Storage, just off Kenner Avenue."

Dominic places another picture in front of LeBlanc. "Do you recognize this picture?"

"No."

Dominic places a third picture in front of LeBlanc. "Do you recognize this picture?"

"Yeah. Her name is Teresa. She came by and got a tattoo from me. I took her out a couple of times."

"You're referring to Teresa Elaine McCall, the girl in the picture?"

"Yeah."

"When did you meet Miss McCall?"

"It was around Valentine's Day. She came in with a friend and got a heart and a crescent-moon tattoo."

"Did you ever run into Morone when she was with you?"

"Yeah, he met her the night we went out. We ran into him at a bar, and he had a drink with us."

"Did you take her home?"

"No, she had her own car. What is this about? We went out twice, and I haven't seen her since."

"Did you know that Miss McCall was murdered on March 13 at her apartment?"

LeBlanc stares at Dominic as if in shock. His hands jerk at the wrist-locking device on the table as he tries to jump up. "I didn't know! You're trying to pin this on me! I didn't kill her! I didn't know she was dead! I want a lawyer! You're not going to pin this on me! Get me a lawyer! I'm through with this!"

Dominic retrieves the photos and closes the file folder. He gets up and knocks on the door to the hall. "Deputy, please take Mr. LeBlanc back to his holding cell."

The deputy removes LeBlanc, and Dominic leaves the room. In a few seconds, the control room door opens, and Dominic enters. He thanks the control booth officer, and the officer leaves. Taking a seat next to me, Dominic starts to discuss the interrogation.

"I'm sending a deputy to E-Z Storage on Airline Boulevard. He will call me as soon as he gets inside. This could reveal the missing murder weapon or the pair of gloves that will put the nails into Morone's coffin."

"What's your take on LeBlanc?" I ask. "Do you think Morone acted alone?"

"He appeared to be surprised by the death of Teresa McCall, the third victim. What he knows and doesn't know concerning the murder of the first victim, Elizabeth DeBoy, and his involvement are up to a jury to decide. He will also be charged with selling stolen goods, along with breaking his parole."

"His answers are consistent with the information I obtained on the third victim, Teresa McCall. I think he's telling the truth." I sit silently for a minute as the recent information starts to derail my thoughts on Morone. "I have another interview with Morone in the morning," I say. "Before I came here, I was also able to meet with Mrs. Lane, the mother of Bill Tamboli, Morone's best friend in high school. Bill was killed in 1999. It turns out Morone's real name is Frankie Benson. It was Frankie's stepfather who killed Bill Tamboli in a car crash. His stepfather was under the influence of alcohol at the time of the accident. Shortly after that, Frankie had a breakdown and was admitted to a psychiatric hospital in Memphis. One of the attendants at the hospital was the second victim, Mary Cotton. Mary was also Frankie's date at the senior prom, before his breakdown. It makes sense why LeBlanc didn't recognize her picture. He never knew her."

"I'll need all that information ASAP. That's good work, Mr. Lancer. I have to say, I'm impressed."

"Thanks. I'll write up what I have and send it to your email tonight."

"Great. I've got some paperwork to finish myself. I'll let you know what we find in the storage room. Please turn in your pass before leaving."

By the time I arrive home, it's six o'clock. The day has rocked my self-confidence. How could I have been completely wrong about Morone?

I have to put my feelings aside and concentrate on the report at hand. It takes me several hours to write and rewrite the information before I send it to Detective DeAngelis.

Next, I begin working on the final draft of my article for Rocco at the *Chronicle*. I email him a copy with a note explaining that I have another interview with Morone in the morning and will make some final edits after our encounter.

I think about how I can soften the article, which will be devastating to Mrs. Lane. The more I try, the worse the article becomes. Morone murdered three women that we know of, but I have trouble with Detective DeAngelis's argument that he deserves the death penalty for his crime.

In 2002, the Supreme Court held that executions of mentally impaired criminals are "cruel and unusual punishments" prohibited by the Eighth Amendment to the Constitution. Is the taking of Morone's life justified by his actions? Capital punishment is often defended on the grounds that society has a moral obligation to protect the safety and welfare of its citizens. Murderers threaten others' safety and welfare. Only by putting murderers to death can society ensure that convicted killers do not kill again. In my mind, taking a life when a life has been lost is not justice; it's a form of vengeance and is morally wrong. I recall the 1966 book *In Cold Blood* by Truman Capote. Capote describes the horror of both murder and the death penalty, which he opposed. His book brings to light that through capital punishment, a murder, a horrible crime, is repeated in cold blood.

Trying to clear my mind of my personal feelings, I find myself wanting to meet with Morone's attorney to present the information I have gathered. My hope is that a verdict can be achieved under the statute of the criminally insane. My interview tomorrow may add the pieces he needs to convince the jury. After making some notes for tomorrow, I close my computer and try to get some sleep.

The next morning, I wait for more than an hour before I'm cleared through the jail system to meet with Morone. On this occasion, I'm escorted into the gray cinder block room that contains the glass enclosures. After taking my seat in enclosure number two, I wait for another ten minutes, staring at the black door, which is guarded by a Louisiana deputy.

Once the door opens, Frankie Benson, a.k.a. Raymond Morone, is led into the room. As he shuffles across the floor, I can hear his ankle irons drag over the concrete. His cheekbones protrude on his sunken face. His overall appearance is worse than it was during our first meeting. His head is shaved, and scraggly patches of hair cover his face. Scabs and red discolorations pepper both arms. Dark circles surround his bloodshot eyes, and his lower lip is dark and inflamed.

I pick up the paired phone, and Raymond responds in like manner.

"Raymond, do you remember me?" I ask.

"Yes. Can you help me? They want to burn me." His voice quavers.

"I think I can. But I need to ask you some more questions and meet with your attorney. Are you okay with that?"

"Yes."

"Last time we spoke, you told me about your high school friend Bill Tamboli. Do you remember that?"

"Yes, Bill is my best friend. We're blood brothers. He can't come here to visit me."

I notice Raymond uses the present tense. "I spoke with Bill's mother this week. Do you remember her?"

"Yes, she's nice. She always makes chocolate pie when I come over. I love chocolate pie."

"She told me you and Bill double-dated to the senior prom. Do you remember going to the senior prom?"

"Yes, I remember."

"Do you remember who your date was?"

"No, I didn't have a date."

"What about Bill? Did he have a date?"

"I don't think so. I don't remember anyone."

So far, Morone's posture hasn't changed. He seems relaxed and responsive. I don't notice any jerks or radical eye movement. With his use of the present tense about Bill Tamboli, I steer clear of bringing up Bill's death currently and try to keep him responding to positive memories.

"Did Mrs. Tamboli make you chocolate pie when you lived at the farmhouse in Picayune?" I ask.

"Yes, she is nice to me."

"Did Bill and his mother live there too?"

"No, just me."

His answer deviates from the information I've found in my investigation: it was the Tambolis who lived at the farmhouse. I'm starting to see where he's blocking past memories or suppressing them. His reaction could also have to do with his treatment at the psychiatric hospital.

"Did Bill come over to the farmhouse when you lived there?" I ask.

"Yes, we'd go fishing in the pond behind the house or play in the woods. He liked coming over," he replies.

"Bill's mother told me you got sick after graduation and had to go in the hospital. Do you remember going to the hospital?"

His body shifts, and his head drops. I've hit a nerve. He remains silent and doesn't answer the question.

Finally, he says, "We built a tree house once, but it didn't last long. The wind and rain tore it down."

The questioning is not getting me anywhere, so I decide to push the envelope. "I understand that you like astronomy. Is that true?"

Raymond flinches before he answers. "Yes."

"Do you know the name Lester Miron? He stayed with your grandparents in Hammond. I think he taught science and astronomy."

Raymond leans back in his chair to distance himself and looks around the room. "They need to paint this room. It's dirty."

"Lester Miron died in a barn accident. Do you remember that day?"

Raymond laughs and makes eye contact. "That's crazy. Lester isn't dead. Why would you say that?"

"That's what I heard," I reply.

"That's not true. Lester is fine."

"Is anyone trying to hurt Lester?"

"Yes, there're some bad people trying to kill him, but I won't let them."

"Who are these people?"

"They're bad people! They want to put him in a grave!" He raises his voice.

"Why do they want to do that?"

"Because he's free, and they want to put him in hell!" he shouts.

After his second outburst, the guard at the door speaks up. "Calm down, Raymond, or I'll take you back to your cell."

Raymond takes a deep breath and shifts in his seat.

"Are these bad people like demons from hell?" I ask.

"Yes, like that," he answers.

"Do you know the name Frankie Benson?"

Raymond rocks back and forth in his chair as he looks away. "No!" he shouts.

"Is your real name Frankie Benson?"

"I'm Raymond Morone! I'm Raymond Morone! I'm Raymond Morone!" he yells.

The guard immediately pushes a red button beside the door. In a matter of seconds, another deputy rushes in. It takes both guards to overpower Raymond and drag him out of the room. The whole time, he keeps yelling, "I'm Raymond Morone! I'm Raymond Morone!"

As soon as I leave the jailhouse, I get a call from Rocco at the *Chronicle*.

"What's all this crap about capital punishment in your article? What are you trying to do? This guy is a murderer. Readers don't want this crap. They want justice."

"In my opinion—"

Rocco cuts me off. "I don't give a damn about your opinion. I just want the facts about the murders. I want something the readers can get enraged about. You must excite their passion. I want them to scream for blood. That's what sells copies."

"I just want to present all the information. The man is sick and needs help."

"Yeah, save somebody else. This man is a serial killer. If you can print the truth or a shady story, you print the story. That's what the readers want. Let them draw their own conclusions."

Taking a deep breath, I ask the question: "What do you want me to do?"

"Nothing. I'll take care of it. Keep your mind on what sells, and in the future, keep your opinions to yourself."

The phone goes dead. I'm mad enough now to push redial and tell Rocco that if he changes my article, he'll have to take my name off it, because I quit. My next thought is about Kate. I realize I'd better get another job before cashing in, but I will insist that he take my name off the article. I'll deal with that in person.

My next move is to leave a message for Raymond's attorney. I explain who I am and say I have valuable information concerning Raymond Morone that'll be pertinent to his trial.

As I drive toward Jackson Square, Raymond's lawyer returns my call. After a short discussion of the investigative material in my possession, he agrees to meet with me later.

Needing to take a break, I park behind Jackson Square and take a stroll over to the Riverwalk. Finding an empty bench facing the river, I sit down and try to gather my thoughts. I know that siding with Raymond's attorney will be the end of any relationship with Detective DeAngelis, and standing up to Rocco will end my current employment. The thought of changing my whole life in the coming week is overwhelming. I feel suffocated and alone, almost to a point of depression. Just when I'm about to start a self-invited pity party, a familiar voice jerks me back to reality.

"Hello, Mr. Lancer. I'm surprised to find you here this time of day. May I join you?"

John the Baptist is a welcome sight. He's dressed in a bright yellow T-shirt with "John 3:16" printed on the front. His faded shorts are frayed at the bottom and are held up by a pair of red suspenders. His traditional rope and cross dangle around his neck. His smile and tattered Bible establish his spirit.

"Absolutely. Please sit down. It's good to see you. I hope you're doing well."

"I'm doing very well. Thank you, Mr. Lancer. And how is your day going?"

"Not so well, John. I'm caught between a rock and a hard place."

"Oh yes. That time when we need to make a decision and question what is best. I always look at what is right and not the anticipated effect. We humans are strange creatures. We're given an amazing brain with the ability to think ahead and plan. But what's so odd is that we spend more time worrying about what we think may happen but never does. In those cases, it's better to follow your heart than your brain. Worry causes procrastination. And with procrastination, no decision is made. Yes indeed, we're really strange creatures."

I sit for a minute as I consider John's words. John interprets my silence correctly, and we both stare at the river without speaking.

"You know, John, you're right. I have a beautiful lady I proposed to this week, and my future is with her. I'll start a new life and a new career. I'll find another employer and share the information I've accumulated in the hope that it will make a difference in a man's life. I just hope I'm not too late."

"Mr. Lancer, it's never too late to do what is right." John smiles. "And congratulations on your engagement. That's wonderful news. If you're looking for a new writing career, I have a friend who is the publisher of the *Clarion Herald*, the official newspaper of the Archdiocese of New Orleans. It's the outlet for editorials by the archbishop and publishes articles on controversial subjects, such as abortion, capital punishment, homelessness, and social issues that exist in the different parishes.

"The *Clarion* started in 1963 and was the successor to the *Catholic Action of the South,* which was published for more than thirty years in the New Orleans area. I haven't seen their circulation numbers in a long time, but in 1965, it was listed in the House Congressional Records at one hundred twenty-five thousand. That was the same year it was honored for a series of articles on the problem of poverty in New Orleans. It's a grand newspaper. My friend told me this morning that he's desperately in need of an investigative reporter. Is that something you may be interested in?"

"John, that's exactly what I'm looking for."

"Excellent, Mr. Lancer! I'll give my friend a call and let him know you'll contact him. I wouldn't wait too long. He said he needs to quickly fill the position."

"It will be done today, and thank you."

John stands and excuses himself. "You're very welcome, Mr. Lancer, and congratulations again on your engagement."

Feeling refreshed, I give Kate a call. She overflows with excitement about her new position at Tulane. She starts moving into her office next week. I explain to her what has transpired with Rocco and the *Chronicle.* She listens silently and allows me to finish before speaking. She agrees with my decision and is fascinated by my opportunity at the *Clarion Herald.* We decide to meet in the morning to look for rings and grab lunch in City Park.

After hanging up, I head home to accomplish a few items. I need to send Raymond's attorney the information I have and send my résumé to the publisher at the *Clarion Herald.* I plan to call my parents to inform them of my decision to change jobs and discuss with Mom my last interview with Frankie Benson, a.k.a. Raymond Morone.

My thoughts are interrupted by a call from Detective DeAngelis. He informs me that a roll of nylon rope and several pairs of welding gloves were found in the E-Z Storage unit registered to Raymond Morone. The rope and gloves have been turned over to forensics and will be processed through the coroner's office, as before. A match of either one will certainly close the case.

By the time I reach home, I'm exhausted. After making a pot of coffee, I spend the next hour organizing the computer information I have on Morone to email to his lawyer. I stare at the Send button, knowing this single action will change my life. John's words echo in my mind: "It's never too late to do what is right." I smile and push the button.

Next, I pull up the website for the *Clarion Herald*, gather the needed information, and then update my résumé and email it with a cover letter to the publisher.

I wait thirty minutes and then call the paper. I'm connected to the publisher, who is surprised and excited to hear from me. He says that he has spoken with John and that I come highly recommended. Commenting on my résumé, he asks if I have time today to stop by for an interview. After accepting his offer, I clean up and head his way.

On my way to the *Clarion*, I get another call. "What now?" I laugh.

The call is from Eric Nelson at the coroner's office. He tells me the nylon rope found at E-Z Storage matches the fiber characteristics found on the three victims. Furthermore, the leather fibers from one of the pairs of welding gloves match the fibers found under the fingernails of the first victim, Elizabeth Mary DeBoy. He also tells me Raymond Morone is being moved by court order to the East Louisiana Mental State Hospital in Jackson, Louisiana, pending his trial. Eric says the state-operated hospital contains a maximum-security unit that provides evaluation, management, and treatment for psychiatric disorders, including competency issues, and ensures the safety and security of male patients.

After my interview with the publisher at the *Clarion Herald* and a tour of the newspaper facility, I can clearly see myself making this career change. The publisher says he will run my résumé by the archbishop and get back to me with an offer.

I call my parents to inform them about my day and discuss my interview at the *Clarion*. Dad sees the position as an excellent opportunity to further my career while doing something that can truly make a difference in social reform. He comments that Rocco and the *Chronicle* are becoming part of the media whose purpose is to incite readers with misinformation, which can be dangerous. Protests and social unrest are led by propaganda.

Mom offers her assistance to Frankie's attorney if he would like to speak with her concerning Frankie's psychiatric evaluation. We hope the judicial system will place Frankie in an institution for the criminally insane.

Sitting on my back patio, I sip my coffee in total darkness and reflect on the passing years. The crescent moon escapes its bondage and casts its illumination along the wood fence. A lone dove coos from a distant tree. Lightning bugs dance near the ground, searching for a mate. The night seems peaceful and content. The crescent moon hides its face and reminds me of the graveyards where the dust of our fathers is scattered to the wind. Lost is the touch we need so desperately. Lost are the laughs and the tears. I've come to know that death is not the end of a journey but a continuation. Those lost to the gardens of stone walk among us beneath the crescent moon.

To every life there comes a time to reflect on passing years.
Choices made and the paths that led to now.
For every life has a beginning and end.
The present leaves behind no regrets to the roads wandered.
The future roads matter not for the journey.
For my Lord lights my path.
He removes all fear.
He sets my soul at peace.

EPILOGUE

By early April, my new life has started to settle in. Kate and I set a wedding date and plan to have a small gathering of parents and friends over for our engagement party. Both of us have started our new jobs, Kate at Tulane and me at the *Clarion Herald*. Frankie Benson's attorney is confident that with the information I have given him, along with the psychiatric evaluation, Frankie will be covered under the Supreme Court ruling for mentally impaired criminals and protected by the Eight Amendment to the Constitution.

Andre LeBlanc is being held for trial, but no charges are being brought against him for conspiracy to commit murder. Andre's cousin Willy is out on bail but is facing state charges for knowingly harboring a wanted criminal from the authorities.

I speak with Detective DeAngelis, who, after a few choice words, thanks me for my investigation and is glad to close his file on Frankie Benson, a.k.a. Raymond Morone. We end our conversation cheerfully, and he accepts my invitation to the party.

I make a special trip to visit Mrs. Lane, Bill Tamboli's mother, and her sister in Hammond. The visit is heart-wrenching, to say the least. Both ladies become emotional but thank me for the work I've done and for coming by personally to speak with them.

That same afternoon, I go by Café Reconcile to invite John the Baptist to our engagement party. As I approach the front door, I'm confronted by an elderly man. He's nicely dressed and has a small white beard and thinning hair. His face is weather-beaten and cracked. A huge smile invites me in. Around his neck is a rope necklace with a cross hanging from it. His twisted body leans to his right side, supported by a wooden cane.

"You must be Justin Lancer," he says in a deep voice. "John said I'd be seeing you."

"Yes, I'm Justin. I was looking for John. Is he here today?"

"No, John will be out of town for a week or so. He has someone he needs to visit. Is there something I can help you with?" he asks.

"Yes, maybe you can. I just wanted to invite him to my engagement party next Saturday. Can you get a message to him?"

"Yes, I'll be glad to do that. From what he tells me about you, I'm sure he'll be happy to attend. He asked me to give you this envelope. He says you'll know what it's for."

I take the envelope and look inside. It contains a small piece of torn rag, a rope necklace, and a wood cross, the symbols of a ragpicker. As I look up, the elderly man is walking away.

"Thank you, sir. What is your name?" I ask.

"My name is Simon. Simon Potter."

You shall not fear the terror of the night
nor the arrow that flies by day;
Not the pestilence that roams in darkness
nor the devastating plague at noon.
Though a thousand fall at your side,
ten thousand at your right side,
near you it shall not come.
Rather with your eyes shall you behold
And see the requital of the wicked,
Because you have the Lord for your refuge;
you have made the Most High your stronghold.
No evil shall befall you, nor shall affliction come near your tent,
For to his angels he has given command about you,
That they guard you in all your ways.
Upon their hands they shall bear you up,
lest you dash your foot against a stone.
You shall tread upon the asp and the viper;
You shall trample down the lion and the dragon.
Because he clings to me, I will deliver him;
I will set him on high because he acknowledges my name.
He shall call upon me, and I will answer him;
I will be with them in distress;
I will deliver him and glorify him;
with length of days I will gratify him
and will show him my salvation.

—Psalm 91:5–16

Printed in the United States
By Bookmasters